It's not easy for His Royal Highness
to choose a bride, especially if he's torn
between love and duty...

Welcome to

HIS MAJESTY'S MARRIAGE

by

Rebecca Winters and Lucy Gordon

Two exciting, emotional novellas set in the
glamorous world of European royalty!

And if you love royal stories,
look out next month for

THE PRINCE'S PROPOSAL
by
Sophie Weston
Harlequin Romance® #3709

Where an ordinary girl
is forced to pretend to be a princess!

REBECCA WINTERS
LUCY GORDON
His Majesty's Marriage

TORONTO • NEW YORK • LONDON
AMSTERDAM • PARIS • SYDNEY • HAMBURG
STOCKHOLM • ATHENS • TOKYO • MILAN • MADRID
PRAGUE • WARSAW • BUDAPEST • AUCKLAND

ISBN 0-373-03703-1

HIS MAJESTY'S MARRIAGE

First North American Publication 2002.

HIS MAJESTY'S MARRIAGE Anthology
Copyright © 2002 by Harlequin Books S.A.

THE PRINCE'S CHOICE
Copyright © 2002 by Rebecca Winters.

THE KING'S BRIDE
Copyright © 2002 by Lucy Gordon.

CONTENTS

THE PRINCE'S CHOICE

Rebecca Winters

Rebecca Winters is the mother of four who was very excited about the new millennium because it meant another new beginning for her. Having said goodbye to the classroom where she taught French and Spanish, she is now free to spend more time with her family, to travel and to write the Mills & Boon novels she loves so dearly.

Rebecca Winters has been nominated for a Reader's Choice Award for her title *The Faithful Bride* and was previously voted Utah Writer of the Year! You can visit her Web site at www.rebeccawinters-author.com

**Look out for Prince Raoul's best friend's story,
THE BABY DILEMMA, coming next month,
Harlequin Romance® #3710!**

CHAPTER ONE

PRINCE RAOUL MERTIER BERGERET D'ARILLAC levered his tall, ripcord-strong body from the car, and strode across the cobblestone courtyard of the seventeenth-century Swiss château nestled in the forest overlooking Lake Neuchatel.

Despite the lateness of the hour, the early July night felt warm and balmy. Perfect weather for him and his friends to enjoy a relaxing climb in Zermatt over the weekend.

Intent on reaching his newly modernized apartments, a surprise from his mother he could have done without while he'd been away climbing in the Himalayas at the end of spring, he didn't notice a figure had stepped from the shadows of the giant chestnut tree until he heard his name called.

He paused mid-stride and spun around. "Father?"

"I didn't mean to startle you, my boy."

Raoul shook his head and walked toward him. "Why on earth aren't you in bed?"

"I've been waiting for you."

"So I gather. Philippe just got back from Paris this evening. We've been discussing a weekend climb of the Matterhorn's North Face. I'm afraid we lost track of the time."

In the moonlight, Henri Mertier's gaze took in the handsome features of his only child, whose complexion had been darkened to teak by the elements on Everest.

He had nothing but praise for his devoted, hardworking, thirty-four-year-old son who not only was a brilliant banker and businessman in his own right, but possessed all the qualities a father could pray for in his offspring.

Temperate in most things, his son had a passion for climbing when he could get away, and he always handled his relationships with women in a discreet manner.

In truth, Henri was tremendously proud of Raoul. That was why a terrible sadness washed over him when he considered what had to be said now. He knew it was the last news his son wanted to hear.

Almost the same height as Raoul's six-foot-two physique, he put a detaining hand on his shoulder. "Could we talk inside?"

Something important was on his father's mind. "Of course."

Raoul fell in step with his parent as they approached the main entrance to the château. He opened the heavy door, with the D'Arillac coat of arms emblazoned in stained glass, and ushered his father through the great hallway to the library.

"Let's have a drink, shall we? I feel the need of one."

The odd inflection in his tone caused Raoul to study his father's sober expression which couldn't be hidden by his trimmed brown mustache and beard. Only wings of silver at the temples indicated his seventy years of age.

The two men faced each other in front of the hearth with its ancient glazed tiles. Raoul stared at the wonderful man who'd always been his role model. The pale blue eyes held a mixture of sadness and anxiety.

Unsettled by the look, Raoul decided he needed sustenance after all and poured himself what his father was drinking.

"You obviously have something serious to discuss. What is so urgent you couldn't wait until tomorrow to tell me?"

His father shook his head. His hands were clasped in front of him. He rubbed his thumbs together in an attitude of reflection.

"You're familiar with the phrase, 'God's errand'?"

Raoul didn't move a muscle, but something unpleasant twisted in his gut—some premonition of dread. He'd experienced it on several occasions climbing in the Alps during army maneuvers. The sudden crack of sound—then avalanche. Lines darkened his features.

"Say what you have to say, Father," Raoul said with an uncustomary show of impatience. His parent's comment had begun to alarm him.

"This concerns you and the Princess Sophie."

A pregnant silence invaded the booklined room with its ornate hand-carved furniture and inlaid floors. Raoul felt as if someone had put a fist to his abdomen, dead center. He ran long, tanned fingers through his dark blond hair, a trait passed down from his mother.

"I thought we had an understanding that until I turned thirty-six she was a closed subject."

"I'm afraid her father opened it when I received a call from him earlier this evening. He feels Sophie has reached the age where it has become an embarrassment for her to still be single. It seems he insists that the date of your wedding be moved up."

Henri's words extinguished any light coming from his son's piercing blue eyes.

"How soon?"

After a tension-filled pause, "Two months."

The wineglass slipped from Raoul's fingers and shattered against the parquetry. All color drained from his face, leaving his lips whitened. He stood there clenching and unclenching his fists.

Henri's heart went out to Raoul. If anyone understood how his son felt, Henri did. Thirty-five years ago he'd married Raoul's mother, Princess Louise de Bergeret. They had been betrothed from infancy. Fortunately there'd been an initial attraction on both sides and their marriage grew into a love match.

But, lovely as Sophie was, he knew the fire wasn't there for her on Raoul's part. Though he'd had ample opportunity over the years, his son had never sought her company.

"I'm sorry the news is so distressing to you."

Raoul ran trembling hands through his hair one more time. "I've got to be by myself for a while, Father. Excuse me."

He slipped out the doors of the family château and climbed into the forest beyond the estate. He broke into a run as he left the gentler slopes and made his way through the pines clinging to the steeper hillsides overlooking the lake.

By the time he'd reached his destination, his breath was spent. He flung his body facedown into the bed of wild narcissus and gave way to his grief. Time had no meaning as pain continued to rack his body.

Much later, when he rose to his feet on unsteady legs, the stars had faded from their velvet backdrop.

As a pale yellow dawn filled the sky, he let himself back inside his apartment.

Gripping his cellphone with a hand still redolent of narcissus, he rang Philippe.

"Raoul—" he answered in a gravelly voice. "What time is it?"

"Five-thirty. Can you talk?"

"But of course," his voice came back, much stronger than before. "You want me to come there?"

"No. Meet me at the pier. We'll take a ride."

"I'll join you in ten minutes."

A half-hour later Raoul cut the motor of the speedboat. They were far enough away from shore to ensure total privacy. Without preamble he told Philippe about the bombshell his father had just dropped on him.

"*Mon Dieu*— I thought it was several years away yet." The two men faced each other. Philippe clamped a hand on Raoul's shoulder. "You don't have to go through with it."

"That's true," Raoul muttered. "I can be the only Arillac who ever shrank from his responsibilities in five hundred years."

"It isn't fair that a man be born with that kind of a burden. Is it written in stone you must marry the Princess?" When there was no answer forthcoming, Philippe removed his hand. "Forget I said anything."

Raoul's eyes narrowed. "You think I haven't asked myself that question at least once a day since my teens? I prayed that if I put things off long enough Sophie would experience a *coup de foudre* with someone else by now."

Philippe grimaced. "Ever since I've known you, I've hoped *you* would fall for a woman you couldn't live without. But it never happened. Probably because you knew what was expected of you and wouldn't allow yourself to get too involved."

Letting out the breath he'd been holding, Raoul said, "I don't honestly know. The truth is, no woman has ever attracted me so much that I could feel my duty being tested."

"Why couldn't you have had an ambitious brother?"

They eyed each other soulfully. "It didn't happen, Philippe."

His friend shook his head. "How many times have you been with her in the last year, aside from your formal engagement?"

"That was it."

"Unbelievable!" Philippe smacked his forehead. "And how many times before that?"

"You already know. Half a dozen maybe, since our teens."

"And you were never alone with her! That's no foundation for any kind of marriage."

"By the sound of that, I assume you've decided to take my advice and go after Kellie."

Philippe nodded. "I don't see I have a choice. She's become my whole world."

Philippe had confessed to Raoul that last month he'd fallen hard for a woman staying at his parents' estate near Paris. Raoul knew his best friend had been enamoured of several women in the past, but evidently this one, Kellie, was different.

"Do you have any idea how lucky you are to feel that kind of desire and know it's reciprocated?" Raoul bit out fiercely. "If you have *that* going for you, you can make the rest work."

"I've never wanted a woman so much in my life," he admitted in a haunted whisper. "However, this conversation isn't about me. Raoul— I have an idea. Why don't you ask Sophie to join us in Zermatt?"

"What are you talking about?" he demanded incredulously.

"You two need time together away from your families and protocol. Ask her to come to your chalet. We'll all take the cable car to Schwartzsee together. A two-hour hike to the Berghaus shouldn't be too strenuous for her. We could do a less ambitious climb to the summit from the Hornli Ridge. If she doesn't want to climb from there you cou—"

"What do you mean 'if'?" Raoul cut in. "She'd be terrified at the thought."

"That's the whole point, Raoul. If she has any blood running through her veins, it should put the fear in her to consider marrying a total stranger whose passions she could never understand. The rest of us will go on to the top and leave you two alone. Reserve a double room at the hut. It should terrify her even more to discover that she's marrying a man who's not attracted to her in any way—who has no desire to bed her when given the opportunity. You follow me?

"Twelve hours of getting to know the real you will make her realize that neither of you has a damn thing in common. Let her see beneath the veneer to the flesh and blood man who will always be indifferent to her."

Raoul had been listening to his friend. "*Mon Dieu*—if I thought for one moment I could get her to call off our betrothal..."

"Then you could marry the woman you want? *If* she came along?"

The question reverberated in his head. "I don't know." His voice shook. "But it's worth finding out, *mon ami*."

As Philippe's suggestion took hold, the first ray of hope filled Raoul's being with such powerful intensity he leaped to his feet in reaction, almost dumping them both in the calm blue water.

"Mademoiselle?"

While the six girls who boarded during the summer were impatiently waiting for her to finish passing out the afternoon mail, Lee Gresham looked over her shoulder at the maid. "Yes, Bianca?"

"The Princess Sophie de Ramblet is on the phone for you. It's urgent. Madame Simoness said you could take the call in her private office."

"I'll be right there."

Afraid she knew the reason why her best friend insisted she come to the phone, Lee told the girls they could go out on the grounds to relax, then hurried from the foyer of Pensionnat Beau Lac to the headmistress's bureau.

Darting across the Aubusson rug, she reached for the receiver. Out of breath she asked softly, "Sophie?"

"Thank heaven you answered." Her friend sounded beside herself.

"Your parents didn't find out about Luciano, did they?"

"No— This is much worse."

"What's wrong? Are you alone? Can you talk?"

"Yes, but only for a minute," she said in hushed tones. "Mother just left my room. She told me Daddy's upset because I'm not married yet. Apparently he phoned Henri Mertier last night and the matter has been settled. My wedding to Raoul has been brought forward to two months from now!"

"What?" Lee was aghast. "Have you told Luciano?"

"No. Mother was still in here with me when Raoul phoned from Neuchatel. H-he asked me to join him at his chalet in Zermatt on Thursday so we could get better acquainted over the weekend."

"Better acquainted—" Lee blurted. "Don't you mean *introduced?*" Her cheeks went hot. "I'm sorry, Sophie, but this whole thing is so archaic, I can't understand it."

"Do you honestly think I feel any differently?"

Lee bit her lip. "No, of course not. When we boarded together here at Beau Lac years ago, it's ridiculous to think how much I envied you for being a princess. Your betrothal to Raoul sounded like something right out of *Sleeping Beauty.* I just never dreamed the fairy tale would end up a nightmare."

"That's exactly what it is! I don't dare tell Luciano until I can see him in person and explain what's happened."

"How are you going to arrange that? With your marriage imminent, you won't have a moment to yourself."

"This is where you come in, Lee. I've got a plan. I've already arranged for Madame Simoness to give you the time off…"

Naturally. Sophie's parents donated a fortune to the prestigious boarding school in Nyon on Lake Geneva. They were wonderful people who treated Lee like family. Lee was eaten up by guilt because they had no idea how many times she'd helped Sophie and Luciano get together.

"You want me to go to Zermatt with you," she said in a wooden voice. It was a statement, not a question.

"Yes. We'll take the train to Visp, where I'll meet Luciano. You'll go to Zermatt from there on the train and make my excuses to Raoul in person."

Lee tried to swallow, but her mouth had gone dry. "I'd do just about anything for you, Sophie. But to lie to his face—"

"It won't be a lie. I'm already feeling ill. Please, just listen. To avoid the press, he's sending one of his friends named Philippe Didier to pick me up in front of the station and drive me to his chalet. The man will be holding a sign that says 'Miami' so people will think he's waiting for an American tourist."

"But his friend will see right away I'm not *you!*" Lee's panic was bordering on hysteria.

"When you inform him you're there in my place to speak to the Prince, he won't question it. After you reach the chalet, you'll tell Raoul I became nauseous on the train and took the next one back to Geneva."

"That's it?"

"No. There's one more thing I need you to do for me. It's the last thing I'll ever ask of you, I promise."

How many times had Lee heard that before?

Knowing this was Sophie, the girl who in the past had got into more trouble than any other boarder at the school, Lee had the distinct impression she wasn't going to like what her friend was about to suggest. The back of her neck started to prickle.

By the time Sophie had finished explaining her plan, perspiration had broken out on Lee's body. "You actually *want* me to come on to him?"

"Yes. Please do it for me! You've seen pictures of him

and know how attractive he is; it won't be so hard. If my own best friend can tempt him to spend the weekend with her then I'll go to my parents and tell them I refuse to marry a man who can't even be faithful to me eight weeks before the wedding!

"If they want proof, you'll be able to provide it. My parents love and trust you like a daughter. To hear the truth from your lips will appall them, and Daddy will call off the wedding. It *has* to be my father who calls it off, Lee." Her voice trembled. "It's the *only* legitimate way the betrothal can be broken. After I've gone through a suitable period of grief, I'll introduce them to Luciano."

"Sophie—you haven't thought this through. Raoul will call the château to find out your condition and discover you're not there!"

"Not if you give him my cellphone number. Then it won't matter where I am. I'll think of something to tell my parents so it won't alarm them if he does call Geneva to check up on me."

By now Lee was shaking, because it was impossible to say no to Sophie. "And what am *I* supposed to do if His Royal Highness decides he wants to enjoy a weekend affair with me?"

"Knowing you, you'll think of a gracious way to get out of it."

"You mean I'm to blow hot, then cold?"

"Exactly."

"What if he's not a gentleman?"

"Then I need to find that out too! I'm sure you'll know how to handle him. You weren't the most brilliant girl in school for nothing! I'll reserve a room for you at the Belle-Vue in Zermatt. I'm sure you could use a few days' vacation. Who knows? While you're walking around, you might even meet a man who'll help you put the past away.

It will give us a lot to talk about on Sunday when I join you for the return trip to Geneva.''

Lee shook her head in despair. ''I don't think I can go through with this, Sophie.''

''But you must! There's only one man I want to marry, and—*oh, la la*, someone's coming. I have to hang up now. A car will be waiting for you outside the school at ten on Thursday morning to take you to the train station. We'll meet on board. *À bientôt, ma chère copine.*''

CHAPTER TWO

LUCIANO BERNALDI placed Lee's suitcase inside the train, then gave her a fierce hug. "Thank you for helping us," he whispered in heavily accented English. "I'm counting on you."

Lee shivered at the remark which had come straight from his heart.

After he stepped back on the platform to pull Sophie into his arms again, the two of them waved to Lee until the train moved out of the station. Once they'd disappeared, she picked up her suitcase and found a seat inside.

Sophie's Swiss boyfriend lived in Ascona, a town in the Italian canton of Ticino. Though he came from a family of wealthy hoteliers, he held no title and could never be on a par with Raoul. The prestigious House of D'Arillac had prevailed over the Frenchspeaking cantons for centuries.

The year before, the two of them had met by chance while Sophie and Lee were vacationing at one of the Bernaldi hotels on Lake Maggiore. When the lift had stuck because of a brief power outage Sophie, who feared heights, had become very frightened.

It was Luciano himself, with his black hair and aquiline features, who had rescued them. Lee might as well have been nonexistent because he and Sophie had fallen for each other on the spot. Over the last twelve months their feelings had deepened until they could hardly bear to be apart.

The man had been begging Sophie to marry him, but she was torn because she loved her parents and couldn't stand to go against their wishes. Many times Lee had tried to put herself in Sophie's place, but couldn't. All she knew was that if she were the one madly in love, she'd probably forget her title and run off with Luciano.

But maybe she could say that so easily because she'd lost all sense of family when her parents and fiancé had been killed. That had been three years ago, a long enough time to stop actively grieving.

At the funeral, Lee's aunt and uncle from West Yellowstone, Montana, had offered her a home with them. But Sophie had begged Lee to return to Switzerland where she could continue to live and work near her. She'd argued that Madame Simoness needed her, not to mention the girls at the school who would help her forget her pain.

In the end, Lee had chosen to go back to Nyon. Between everyone there, especially Sophie's parents, she had been able to make it through that agonizing period. Now, sadly, Sophie was asking something of Lee that seemed such a betrayal of the Ramblets's love and caring.

By the time the train reached the station in Zermatt, she could hardly breathe for the tension that constricted her chest. When the train emptied, she found herself in the middle of a crowd that swept her along the platform to the entrance.

She couldn't have arrived on a more beautiful, brisk afternoon. The last time she'd stayed here overnight, with the boarders from the school, clouds had obscured the Matterhorn. Today it rose in the distance like a giant snow-covered sentinel, overlooking the lush green valley dotted with chalets and hotels.

The sight was so beautiful Lee could hardly believe it was real. But her appreciation was short-lived the moment she saw the "Miami" sign held by a lanky male in dark trousers and a windbreaker.

That would be Philippe, Raoul's friend. He stood in front of one of those electric cars, the only kind allowed in

Zermatt. She thought he looked very French and attractive in his own way, with overly long dark hair and hooded eyes. While his gaze swept the crowd for signs of Sophie, it managed to linger on Lee in male appreciation several times in the process.

With her cap of silvery-gold curls and violet eyes, she'd become used to the stares of men, especially the dark-haired types living in Europe and the Middle East. But to capture the interest of Prince Raoul was something else again.

Hoping her legs would support her, she walked toward the man. "Hello, Philippe," she said in English. Might as well play the part of the American tourist to make everything real.

His black eyes gleamed with flattering interest. "Hello," he responded in kind with a French accent. "Have we met before?"

"No, we haven't. But my best friend told me you would answer to that name and be carrying a sign I would recognize. If we could get in the car, I will tell you everything."

Her explanation wiped the lazy amusement from Philippe's expression. After eyeing her speculatively, he opened the car door for her. Once he'd helped her inside, he stashed the sign and her bag, then went around to the driver's side and slipped behind the wheel.

He studied her as if she were a puzzle that needed solving. "Who are you?"

"My name is Lee Gresham. I'm a close friend of Princess Sophie."

The lie was about to begin.

"She asked me to accompany her to Zermatt, but she became ill on the train and was forced to return to Geneva. I wanted to go back with her, but she hated disappointing

Prince Raoul and begged me to see him in person so I could tell him what happened.''

His body remained motionless, yet she could tell something of significance was going on inside him.

''Do you mind taking me to his chalet?''

''No, no. Of course not,'' he hastened to assure her, but his thoughts had been far away. After a moment he started the car and they were off.

She sat nervously in the seat, frightened to see that, so far, Sophie's plan was going exactly as she'd outlined.

He drove to the outskirts of the world-famous Swiss village. From there the road wound up into a flowering hillside where she spied a small, charming brown and white chalet with an outside staircase that led to the top story. There were two other cars in the parking area.

Before Philippe could come around to assist her, a man had emerged from the back entrance of the house. Lee would have known the Prince anywhere.

From the time she'd first arrived at boarding school in Nyon she'd seen his picture in the newspapers and magazines. It was no secret that she, along with the other boarders, had pretty well worshipped him the way many teens idolized a famous film or rock star.

After she'd become friends with Sophie, and found out she was betrothed to him, Lee had gone through a period of coveting Sophie's future intended. But that destructive emotion had ended when Lee met Todd and fell in love.

They would be married right now except for the tragedy that had shattered her life and made her view the world through different eyes.

Having lost everyone close to her, Lee took Sophie's love affair with Luciano seriously. The two were so besotted it seemed criminal that an accident of birth was forcing Sophie to marry a man for whom she had no feelings. Lee had determined to help them in any way she could.

But talking about Prince Raoul in the abstract was one thing. Meeting him in person for the first time was an entirely different matter.

Beneath the natural gold highlights of his dark blond hair blazed a pair of eyes so hot a blue they rivaled flame. Lines of character and intelligence were carved in a rugged face tanned to mahogany by the elements. He stood at least six feet two inches of lean muscle.

As he approached the car, her heart raced at the impact of his virile masculinity. For sheer physical appeal, he made every male she'd ever met before look inadequate by comparison.

Sophie had to be a different species of female not to have fallen for Raoul on sight!

Closer now, she saw him blink when he realized a total stranger was sitting next to Philippe. He opened the door and lowered his head.

Their eyes met in a long searching glance.

In the heart-stopping silence a thorough scrutiny seemed to be taking place on both sides. Lee was so mesmerized she couldn't look away. *This* was the man she was supposed to—

"Raoul?" Philippe interjected, causing her to remember why she was here. "This is Lee Gresham, a close friend of Sophie's," he explained in English. "Ms Gresham? This is Raoul Mertier."

"H-how do you do, Your Highness." She stumbled over the words, feeling as foolish as any starstruck schoolgirl meeting her ultimate fantasy.

"Call me Raoul." He spoke English with barely a trace of accent in a deep voice she found as attractive as the rest of him.

"Oh—" Her heart was pounding with a fury that made her feel breathless. "Sophie would be here if she hadn't become n-nauseous on the train and—"

"Why don't you come inside the chalet where we can talk?" he interrupted smoothly and helped her from the car. By accident their bodies brushed against each other as he leaned inside to retrieve her bag. She felt as if she'd just come up against a live wire.

Without waiting for him, she hurried toward the house, knowing she couldn't possibly follow through with a plan that had been flawed from the beginning. One look into those brilliant blue depths of his and she'd realized he wasn't a man to be trifled with.

This wasn't going to work. She knew it wasn't!

As soon as she'd explained about Sophie she would ask to be driven to the hotel where she would phone her friend and tell her she couldn't go through with the plan.

Raoul managed to beat her to the entrance. "This way," he murmured, holding the door open for her. On a shaky whisper she said thank you and moved past him, aware her five feet five inches wouldn't seem very tall to him. Then she chastised herself for thinking any personal thoughts at all.

"Would you care to freshen up in here first?" He'd stopped outside a door halfway down the corridor.

"No, I'm fine. Thank you anyway."

She felt his gaze travel over her in swift appraisal before he led her to the front room which gave out on a superb view of the storybook surroundings. He placed her bag against the wall.

To her surprise the interior of the chalet was rustic rather than luxurious. The perfect paradise for a skier, with its huge grate hearth and large, comfortable couches made for lounging. There was a set of double doors leading to the dining room. At the end of the living room she noticed a staircase which led to what looked like a loft.

Philippe seemed to have disappeared.

Her palms grew damp. Ill at ease, she rubbed them

against her hips covered by her black cotton sweater and matching wool pants. It was an outfit Sophie had insisted made the most of Lee's voluptuous curves and coloring.

Dear God— What was she doing here alone in this chalet with Sophie's fiancé? This was madness! Prince or not, he was a man first. One who deserved all the honesty she had in her.

He stood in the center of the room with his legs slightly apart. She noted he had a bearing as splendid as his title. "May I offer you a drink or something to eat?"

She shook her head. "That's very kind of you, but no."

"Then sit down and tell me what happened."

Averting her eyes, so she wouldn't get caught staring at him again, Lee did his bidding. "Sophie asked me to come on this trip with her. Quite soon after we left Geneva she started to feel ill. She couldn't decide if she'd eaten something that didn't agree with her, or if she was coming down with the flu. Finally she alerted her parents that she was returning home and got off the train. When I talked to her a little while ago someone had already picked her up, so I know she's in good hands."

Hoping that lightning wouldn't strike her, she continued, "Sophie refused to let me go back with her. She said it was vital I deliver her regrets to you in person because she hated disappointing you."

He rubbed his chest in an unconscious gesture. "More than anything, I'm sorry she was distressed enough to have to return home."

He sounded so sincere Lee found herself loathing this untenable situation. "The thing is, she knew you would have gone to a lot of trouble to make elaborate plans for her. Naturally she didn't feel that a phone call would suffice. If you'd like to contact her now, I'll give you her cellphone number, but I would imagine she's resting at the moment."

No doubt Sophie was consoling herself in Luciano's arms while they waited for Lee to carry out a scheme destined for failure. No matter how much she wanted to help them, she couldn't take this charade any further.

Lee wrote the phone number down on a piece of notepaper from her handbag and placed it on the coffee table. Unable to sit still, she got to her feet and finally dared to look at him once more.

"I—I don't know what else to say except that I can assure you she's very sorry. Depending on her condition, I'm sure you'll hear from her in the morning, if not tonight. Now, if I could prevail on your friend Philippe to drive me to the Belle-Vue, I'd be grateful."

His hand stilled against his solid chest. "You're meeting someone there?" he questioned.

"Oh, no. It's a place to stay for the night before I return to Nyon tomorrow." No more lies.

His veiled eyes studied her upturned features. "What's in Nyon?"

"The boarding school where I live and work."

"It wouldn't be Beau Lac, would it?"

She nodded. "Sophie and I both attended it for several years. While we were there we became best friends. I stayed on and obtained my university degree in Geneva. Now I'm one of the staff."

He moved closer, filling her with a fluttery sensation. "Where are you from in America?"

Oddly enough she got the impression he wasn't making polite conversation. He sounded as if he really wanted to know. She couldn't understand why he was asking so many questions.

"Jackson, Wyoming."

His eyes flared a darker blue. "I've been there. That's some of the most beautiful country I've ever seen."

He had the most beautiful eyes she'd ever seen.

"I thought it was paradise until I saw pictures of the Swiss Alps for the first time. When I was old enough to climb the Grand Teton with my father, I pretended I was on the Matterhorn."

The slow smile that broke the corners of his mouth reached his eyes, illuminating dark places in her soul where she'd thought the light had been extinguished forever.

"Did you find goats and hear yodeling?"

She chuckled in spite of her nervousness. "I'm afraid not."

"Have you ever been up on the Matterhorn?" came the silken inquiry.

"No," she whispered, fighting tears because her father had promised it would be their next climb. But that had been right before everything ended...

A strange tension hovered between them.

"How would you like to spend your weekend climbing it with me?"

CHAPTER THREE

SUDDENLY Lee felt the room tilt. Sophie's words came back to haunt her.

If my own best friend can tempt him to spend the weekend with her, then I'll go to my parents and tell them I refuse to marry a man who can't even be faithful to me eight weeks before the wedding!

Except that Lee hadn't tempted him! In fact she'd gone out of her way to do just the opposite.

Shaken to the foundations by his invitation, she was thrown into a new morass of conflicting emotions.

Part of her was in pain for Sophie, who'd already suspected that Raoul might be unfaithful to their engagement, not to mention their marriage. Already Lee had proof that the Prince felt no compunction in replacing Sophie with the next available female.

Unfortunately there was another part of Lee inexplicably drawn to the exciting male standing too close to her. More than anything she wanted to say yes to him.

It didn't matter that Sophie had given Lee permission to entice her fiancé into a weekend tryst. The fact that he'd jumped at the opportunity without any machinations on Lee's part meant that if he and Sophie were forced to marry, their union would be disastrous for them and any children born to them.

Angry at herself, at Sophie, at him, she blurted, "Is *that* what you were planning to do with the Princess?"

Raoul felt strong emotion coming from those gorgeous eyes flashing purple sparks at him. Obviously his invitation had surprised her as much as it had him. But now that it was out he had no desire to take it back.

The moment Philippe had returned with the breathtaking stranger Raoul had realized his carefully laid plans to put Sophie off the idea of marrying him were dashed for the time being.

At this point he was intrigued to know why she'd sent this American woman to make a personal apology. Sophie could have phoned him with her excuses. Something didn't add up...

"The answer to your question is 'yes'," he answered honestly. "I thought she might like to share one of my favorite sports with me."

Her beautiful body stiffened. "Climbing the Matterhorn isn't exactly like playing a set of tennis. If you'd bothered to get to know Sophie better you'd understand she has a terrible fear of heights."

Raoul was taken aback. Where was all this anger coming from? She sounded like a mother lion defending her cub.

"Is that why the Princess sent you in her place? Because she knows you don't have the same problem?"

Those heavenly eyes stared straight into his. "I'm afraid her mind wasn't on mountain climbing."

His gaze narrowed on her passionate mouth. "You're sure about that?"

"I'd stake my life on it," she bit out. "Otherwise she would probably have suggested you meet her in Geneva."

A tiny nerve was hammering at the base of her throat. What flawless skin she had.

"Apparently the Princess doesn't have a problem sending her best friend to fill in for her."

"What are you insinuating?"

"Give me a little credit, Ms Gresham. You wouldn't have arrived with some fairy tale about having climbed the Grand Teton unless you'd done your homework first."

Hectic color stained her cheeks. "It sounds like you believe what the tabloids say about the thousands of female admirers who follow your every move and know everything down to the brand of shampoo you use. Give *me* a little credit for not being part of the adoring horde!"

She wheeled away from him and reached for her suitcase.

Stunned by her fiery reaction, Raoul blocked her path so she couldn't escape down the hallway.

"Not so fast," he cautioned, putting his hands on her shoulders so she couldn't turn and run out the front door. His hands scorched where they held her.

Lee froze in place, remembering another conversation with Sophie.

What if he's not a gentleman?

Then I need to find that out too. I'm sure you'll know how to handle him. You weren't the most brilliant girl in school for nothing.

Right now Lee wasn't sure of anything. She'd been playing with fire and had let her temper get the best of her. As a result, he held her in his firm grasp, almost daring her to take another step.

With his powerful male body so close she could feel its warmth and smell the fresh scent of the soap he used; she was blinded to the issue at hand. This was so much worse than anything she'd imagined. Especially when she was guilty of almost everything he'd accused her of without realizing it.

"I'm afraid you and I have gotten off on the wrong foot," he began in his deep compelling voice. His hands seemed to slide away from her upper arms with reluctance. "If it's all right with you, I'd like to start over."

Chastened by his conciliatory tone and her own guilt, she backed away from him. "I-it's my fault," she faltered. "I've lived around Sophie long enough to understand why you're both suspicious of strangers. You had every right to think and say the things you did. Please tell me you forgive me, then I can leave feeling a little better.''

She heard his sharp intake of breath. ''What if I don't want you to go?''

Lee blinked in shock.

''You admit you've accomplished your errand and have little else to do but wait in an empty hotel room until tomorrow. If you would enjoy a good climb, then why not go up on the mountain with me and my friends in the morning? The guys will love it.''

Now what was he saying?

Something was terribly wrong here. She wasn't supposed to wish that Raoul had said *he* would love it. The man certainly wasn't the person Lee had thought he was a few minutes ago. He sounded...honorable.

It was more than apparent that Sophie didn't know anything about the real Raoul. Swallowing hard, Lee said the first thing on her mind. ''What about Sophie?''

He reached for the paper Lee had put on the table. ''I'll phone her right now. If she's feeling better, I'll call off the climb and fly to Geneva in the morning to see her. Since you're her best friend, naturally I'll take you back with me. Excuse me for a moment.''

In a few strides he reached the stairs, which he took three at a time. Lee noted he moved with the grace of a natural athlete. She let go of her suitcase and sank down on the nearest couch, closing her eyes as if to shut out her fears.

Somehow he'd turned things around, making it difficult for her to back out if she didn't want him to think she'd lied about everything.

Worse, as soon as he talked to Sophie she would be so overjoyed to discover her plan was working she'd pretend to be ill for the entire weekend and encourage him to entertain Lee.

That meant she would be spending the next few days in Raoul's company. It appeared that one of her teenage fantasies about being with him was going to come true. Except that in her dreams they'd been strictly alone, and there had been no princess...

Upstairs in the spacious loft, where there were four beds, Raoul spoke with Sophie while Philippe stood nearby. After telling her they'd make other plans once she had recovered, he clicked off the cellphone and stared at his friend.

"What's going on?" Philippe demanded.

Raoul shook his head. "I wish I knew. Sophie says she's feeling very sick."

"Do you believe her?"

"I don't know. Philippe—do you think it's possible she's as horrified over the marriage date being brought forward as I am?"

He shrugged his shoulders in typical Gallic fashion. "I suppose anything is possible. Is that why you invited her best friend to join us on the climb? To see if you could learn the truth from her?"

Raoul looked away, but not fast enough to fool his friend.

"I knew it," Philippe cried. A wicked smile broke out on his face.

"What do you think you know?" he muttered in irritation.

"I saw the way you were looking at each other out by the car. *Mon Dieu*—with all that energy you two could have lit up a whole city!"

"You're jumping to conclusions," Raoul retorted, raking a hand through his hair in frustration.

"No, my old friend. I have eyes in my head. I know what I saw, what I felt. You've just discovered what it's like to be struck by the *coup de foudre*. She's what the Americans call a knockout.''

''You mean like Kellie?''

Philippe's head reared back. The two men stared at each other. *''Touché.''*

Raoul didn't need his buddy to tell him what he already knew. Between Lee's lovely face and coloring, and the alluring shape of her body, he was forced to admit he felt an overwhelming attraction to her. But it was more than that.

While she'd stood her ground defying him, giving him as good as she got, something had happened to him on a much deeper level. Something he couldn't explain. All he knew was that he couldn't let her go just yet.

''Do me a favor?''

''Anything,'' Philippe murmured.

''This close to the wedding I can't afford for the *paparazzi* to catch me alone with Lee. Would you mind taking her to the Bergsteig Hof right now to get her outfitted for the climb?''

He grinned. ''It will be my pleasure.''

''Don't enjoy it too much.'' The warning came out before Raoul realized how that sounded.

Philippe shook his head in amazement. ''I never thought I'd see the day when you would say something like that to me. You're not the same man I left an hour ago to go pick up the Princess.''

''I'm not sure what I am,'' Raoul confessed. ''Come on back with her when you're through and we'll eat here tonight before going to bed.''

''That sounds interesting.''

''She'll stay downstairs in the master bedroom, of course.''

''Of course,'' Philippe imitated him in cruel delight. ''Have you informed her of all your plans?''

''I'll do it now.''

"Do you think she has ever set foot on a mountain?"

"I guess we'll find out tomorrow."

If she'd lied to him, then she wasn't the woman Raoul thought she was, and he'd be able to walk away from her without looking back. But, even as he reasoned that way, the idea that she might have been toying with him sent a feeling of desolation through him he couldn't account for.

Tormented by thoughts that could get him into serious trouble, he headed downstairs with Philippe. As they made their way, the sound of voices drifted toward them. It appeared Yves and Roger were back from town and had become sidetracked by the latest arrival.

The eager expressions on their burnished faces revealed how enthralled they were with the charming blond American who spoke impeccable French.

Raoul had seen his climbing buddies in action too many times before and recognized the signs of infatuation. But, to his chagrin, this was one time when he didn't find it amusing.

"It looks like everyone is acquainted." He broke in on their conversation without the slightest compunction. All heads swerved in his direction but he only had interest in one unforgettable face.

"Lee? If you'd go with Philippe, he'll take you to get outfitted for tomorrow. While you're gone I'll phone the Belle-Vue and cancel your reservation."

"Oh, bu—"

"It's all right," he interrupted her. "I'd prefer you stay in the guest room here to avoid problems with the press. They'll have heard there was a hotel reservation made in the Ramblet name and be lying in wait."

He felt her hesitation before she murmured, "I'm sure you're right."

"It will be nice to fool them for a change. When you return from town we'll eat, then turn in early."

She looked as dazed as he felt before she got up from the couch to follow Philippe out of the room.

No one spoke until the back door closed. Yves turned to him. "What's going on, Raoul?"

"I heard her tell you the Princess was too sick to come, so now you know as much as I do. Since Mademoiselle Gresham traveled all this distance to deliver the message, I thought the least I could do was invite her on the climb tomorrow."

Roger looked dumbfounded. "She *wants* to come?"

"Let's put it this way. She didn't refuse."

The astonishment on their faces was so comical Raoul would have been amused if these had been other circumstances. But the fact that she hadn't backed out yet raised more troubling questions than it answered.

It didn't help that his pulse raced every time he thought of being in her company for the next few days.

"Excuse me while I tell Greta there'll be five of us eating in tonight."

CHAPTER FOUR

LEE had made other climbs besides the Grand Teton with her father in the Colorado Rockies. She knew what equipment was necessary.

As soon as she and Philippe entered the sporting goods store she proceeded to find the warm clothing and sunglasses she would need. Before her companion could speak for her, she told the older man behind the counter she wanted mountaineering boots with a good profile for crampons.

It didn't take long to be outfitted with the right helmet and harness. Throwing in a pick ax and rucksack with Thermos, she was ready to check out and pulled the credit card from her wallet.

Philippe covered her hand with his, signaling that she should put it away. "This goes on the Mertier account," he murmured to the other man who nodded without asking questions. Obviously the staff here could be counted on for their discretion, a highly prized commodity for royals like Raoul.

But Lee wasn't a person who expected to be taken care of. Her conscience wouldn't allow her to let the Prince foot the bill for everything.

"This equipment is for me," she asserted, removing her hand from beneath his to give the clerk the credit card. "I'll pay for it."

She'd always paid her way with Sophie, and wasn't about to take advantage of Raoul's generosity now. In fact, she'd been having second thoughts about joining him on the climb ever since he'd extended the invitation.

Thanks to Philippe, the business about who would pay for her equipment had served as a wakeup call. She'd be insane to have anything more to do with Raoul!

Unfortunately now was not the time to make a scene by declaring that she'd changed her mind. The only thing to do was wait until she got back to the chalet to inform Raoul. On her way to the train station, she'd return all the equipment.

During their drive back, Philippe remained silent. In fact from the moment he'd learned she was a friend of Sophie's his behavior had become more reserved. As they drove around the back of the chalet she turned toward him, anxious to say what was on her mind.

"Philippe? Would you answer a question for me?"

He shut off the motor before glancing at her. "If I can."

"I get the feeling tomorrow's climb has been ruined for you."

"Not at all!" he came back with surprising force.

"Be honest—how many times has Raoul invited a woman along?"

He pursed his lips. "This will be the first."

"I thought so. And he did it without consulting the rest of you. Look—Sophie and I may be close, but that doesn't place him under any special obligation to me. Since you and I both know this is the last thing he wants, perhaps you could suggest a good way I can get out of it and just go home? I'll return all these things *en route* to the station." *Sophie wouldn't thank her, but Lee couldn't worry about that now.*

"You don't want to come with us?"

"That's not the point!" she retorted, before she realized the mistake she'd made. Heat scorched her cheeks. "I mean— Oh!"

Someone had opened the passenger door where she'd

been resting. If two familiar male hands hadn't caught her arms from behind she would have fallen out.

Raoul helped her to her feet. The heat from the contact of his skin through her sweater distracted her so much she forgot what she was going to say. This time when their gazes collided the impact of those blue eyes was even more startling than before.

"I'm glad you're back. Dinner's waiting. Come. I'll show you to your room first so you can freshen up."

"Thank you." She followed him inside.

Maybe this weakness she felt around him was the result of an empty stomach. This morning she'd awakened without an appetite. Knowing what Sophie expected of her, Lee had only been able to get down about half a sandwich at one of the train stops. She still wasn't hungry.

He showed her to a bedroom off the hallway which kept the rustic flavor of the chalet. "The dining room is through the doors you saw in the front room. A hearty meal is what everyone needs before our climb in the morning."

His eyes were too alive as they wandered over her. She was too aware of him.

Panic-stricken she said, "If you don't mind, I'm afraid I couldn't eat anything."

His brows furrowed. "What's wrong?"

"I think maybe I've come down with the same thing as Sophie. Bed is the only thing that sounds good."

She could tell he didn't know what to believe, but it no longer mattered if he thought she was lying through her teeth about everything. The sooner she got away from him, the better.

"I'll send Greta with a cup of tea."

"Please don't bother your staff. I couldn't tolerate anything right now."

"If you're that sick, let me at least help you to the bed."

"No—" she cried. "I'll be fine. Please go ahead without

me.'' She closed the door while he still stood there, eyeing her with a mixture of concern and something else she couldn't decipher.

Dear God. The guilt.

Deep down she knew she mustn't go with him tomorrow. If she did, it meant her desire to be with him was stronger than her conscience. That good old conscience which was telling her to get away from him and stay away! Where had it been when she'd agreed to help her friend with this wild idea?

Though Sophie and Raoul had led separate lives up to this point, they'd been raised to do their duty. No matter how much they might want to go against their parents' wishes, neither of them had acted on those wants, otherwise there wouldn't have been a formal engagement earlier this year.

After coming to Zermatt to speak to Raoul, Lee was convinced he was a man of honor who would follow through and marry Sophie. As for Sophie, she might be in love with Luciano now, but Lee was equally convinced that, in the end, her friend would submit to the inevitable and become Raoul's wife.

And proceed to fall in love with him.

Lee groaned in pain as she fell across the bed. That was what was tearing her up inside. The knowledge that Sophie had the right to touch Raoul, to get to know him and love him.

Heavens—he was going to be her best friend's husband in eight weeks, and all Lee could think about was how it would feel to lie in his arms!

That was because she'd fantasized about him too much at boarding school. When she really thought about it, she realized that her relationship with Sophie had always included Raoul somewhere in the background.

He'd been lurking in Lee's psyche all these years and

had become far too familiar to her. Her mistake was letting Sophie talk her into this ridiculous plan. Meeting him in person had brought him to heart-throbbing life.

Don't blame Sophie for this, Lee Gresham. You might have wanted to help your friend, but the truth is you wanted to meet the Prince and this was your chance. You're a wicked girl.

More than ever Lee realized she'd barely been functioning since she'd lost her parents and fiancé. Lee hadn't felt really alive until a few hours ago when she'd first laid eyes on Raoul. Perhaps some professional counseling was in order to help her come to terms with the past?

One thing was certain. It was vital she leave Switzerland right away so Sophie wouldn't be able to include her in their wedding plans. The thought of watching them exchange vows in the cathedral with the whole country looking on was anathema to her.

What she needed to do was go back to Jackson and get a life. With the help of her father's attorney she'd retained the small house her family had once lived in. It was rented at the moment, but she could rent something else until it became vacant. Then she'd look for a job.

Tomorrow she'd return to Nyon and tender her resignation to Madame Simoness. With only a handful of girls staying there over the summer, the headmistress could find someone else to cover Lee's duties until a permanent replacement was found.

With that settled in her mind, she took a quick shower and prepared for bed. No sooner had she climbed under the covers than she heard a knock on the door.

"Lee? May I come in?"

At the sound of Raoul's voice she started to tremble. "Yes—" she called out, before sitting up a little and pulling the eiderdown quilt to her chin. He entered the room carrying a mug of tea and crackers which he put on the table by her bed.

To her consternation he placed a hand on her forehead. His touch fueled the fire burning inside her. "You don't feel hot, but I've still half a mind to send for the doctor."

She fought to stifle a moan. "Please don't. I feel better just lying down. I think I'll try that tea after all." To prove she wasn't in critical condition, she reached for the hot liquid.

In the process she forgot she was wearing a nightgown whose shoulder strap had fallen down her other arm, revealing enough to his gaze that he probably thought she was being provocative. A deep blush swept over her as she quickly tried to cover herself and hold her drink at the same time.

He grabbed it before too much spilled, but not without his fingers coming into breathtaking contact with her flesh. It was a brief moment out of time that should never have happened.

"Would you like to try it again?"

She knew he meant the tea but, coming on the heels of that sizzling physical encounter, she couldn't think, let alone function. "I'll drink it later."

The tension between them was painful in its intensity.

"Your illness must have come on suddenly," he said in a husky tone. "Philippe told me you seemed fine at the sporting goods store."

"I—I thought I was all right too. But I know I can't go climbing tomorrow. Please—follow through with your plans and don't mind me. In the morning I'll phone for a taxi to take me to the station."

A long silence ensued. The enigmatic look on his burnished features prevented her from knowing what he was thinking.

"If that's your wish, then I'll ask Greta to keep an eye

out on you. If you need anything, just dial 0 on the phone by the bed and she'll answer. I'll have your promise on that.''

She averted her eyes. ''You have it.''

''Don't worry about your gear. Greta's husband will take it back to the store in the morning.''

''Thank you. You've been especially kind to me. So have your friends. Tell Philippe I appreciated him picking me up and running me around.''

''I'll pass your words along.''

Her heart was hammering so hard she was afraid he could hear it. ''I'm sorry things didn't work out for you and Sophie this weekend, but there will be plenty of others,'' her voice trailed. ''She's a very fortunate woman. I-it's been a privilege to meet you, Your Highness. Take care on the mountain.''

''Sleep well,'' was all he said before he left the room.

Lee fell back against the pillow in the kind of physical and emotional pain only the man you loved could take away.

After spending half the night replaying the day's events in her head until she thought she'd go mad, she sat up and drank the cold tea. She finished off with the crackers and wished she had more.

It was four in the morning, the in-between time that seemed to pass so slowly. Now that she had a plan, she was desperate to put it into action.

Too keyed up to sleep, she dressed in a pair of denims and a dusky blue knit top with long sleeves and a crew neck. All that was left to do was make the bed and pack her bag.

In a few minutes, while she was fastening the lock, she heard the sound of the cars starting up behind the chalet. She left what she was doing and ran over to the window.

Pretty soon she saw headlights as Raoul and his friends made their way down the hillside.

They needed to leave this early to get up on the mountain before anyone else. Without her along, no doubt they'd climb the North Face, the most challenging of the approaches. The four men were seasoned veterans. During her conversation with them she'd learned that Roger was a guide who lived in Zermatt year round.

Though she knew Raoul could take care of himself, there was a part of her that feared for him. The Matterhorn had claimed its share. Even in beautiful weather it was treacherously cold with gale force winds at the top. One misstep and a climber could fall thousands of feet, even experts like the Prince and his friends.

Shuddering at the mere thought, she left her vigil at the window and turned on the bedroom light. She needed her purse so she could get out her cellphone to call for a taxi.

When that was done, she wrote a note of explanation to Greta in French and left it on the table next to the empty mug. "I guess I'm ready," she murmured to herself, looking around the bathroom and bedroom to see if she'd left anything.

It was time to put all thoughts of Raoul away. When she left this chalet she'd be closing the book on that particular fairy tale forever.

After turning out the light, she moved down the hall as quietly as she could so she wouldn't wake Greta or her husband. Lee would wait for the taxi out in back.

The air was cold, but not freezing. Once the sun came up it would warm everything and illuminate this little portion of heaven on earth. Maybe it was just as well she couldn't see the village right now. Better to drive away in the dark and forget such a place existed.

She had to forget such a man existed.

Five minutes went by before she caught the sound of a

motor. Pretty soon she saw headlights. When the taxi rolled into the parking area, she hurried toward it, anxious to get away before the staff were alerted.

"Merci bien," she called out to the driver, who opened her door from the inside and put down the seat so she could stash her suitcase. "To the station, please."

"Oui, Mademoiselle."

Lee climbed inside and shut the door. She started to thank him for coming at this hour, but a gasp escaped when she discovered who sat behind the wheel.

She'd feared Raoul hadn't believed her when she'd come back from town pleading illness. Even so, she never dreamed he would forego the climb with his friends to catch her stealing away in the darkness. He wouldn't have gone to these lengths if he didn't want answers.

CHAPTER FIVE

RAOUL started up the car and headed out of the parking area. "I'm glad to see you're feeling better."

She fought for a steady breath. "I guess all I needed was some sleep."

"It appears to have done wonders for you. I wish I had been so lucky," his voice grated.

Lee kneaded her hands, waiting for him to say something else, but he kept her in misery during the drive down to the village.

"Y-you've passed the train station."

"It's too early for the train. We're going someplace where we can be warm and completely alone."

This was the very thing she'd tried so hard to avoid.

"Look, Raoul—I don't blame you for being disappointed, even angry because Sophie couldn't make it."

He flashed her an oblique glance. "If you knew me better, you'd realize anger doesn't begin to cover what I'm feeling."

Leaving her to digest the ramifications of that remark, he drove to the other end of the village and pulled around the side of an apartment building.

"This is Roger's condo. There's no cook or caretaker here."

She bowed her head. He'd really meant it when he said they were going to be alone.

After pulling out her suitcase, he helped her from the car. Cupping her elbow, they climbed a flight of stairs. Raoul put the key in the lock and opened the door for her.

If she could be grateful for one thing, it was that it was

still dark out. There were no *paparazzi* around to take pictures of them. She could imagine tomorrow's headlines labeling the blond mystery woman Prince Raoul's latest lover. It would help Sophie's case with her parents, but Lee couldn't imagine a worse punishment.

Roger had left a lamp on. His place contained the same rustic feel as the chalet. However the dozens of pictures, some including Raoul, had turned it into a home.

Over at the entertainment center she noticed a pile of video cassettes on top of Roger's VCR. The label on the top one caught her attention.

"You climbed Everest this year!"

"In the spring," came the deep voice behind her.

"Th-that's incredible. I'd like to see it."

"Perhaps after breakfast."

Not wanting Raoul to get anywhere near her, she moved out of the way and took off her jacket, laying it over a chair. There was an odd gleam in his eyes as he studied her actions.

Frightened that he could read her mind, she blurted, "You obviously brought me here for a reason. Please—" She swallowed hard. "Tell me what it is you want to know."

"I think we'll save that until we've eaten. The kitchen is beyond the archway. After you."

Lee didn't need to be urged. She was famished and Raoul knew it. Besides, the way she was feeling right now, the kitchen was a much safer place for the two of them.

As it turned out, the small dining nook provided enough space for two people. He told her to sit down at the drop table and he'd serve her.

It was her turn to watch him navigate the room. He pulled things out of cupboards and the refrigerator as if he were at home, evidence of a long-term friendship with Roger.

Seeing him like this, you'd never know he came from a titled European family that had specific expectations passed down from father to son. The life of Prince Raoul was one of privilege. That made him forbidden to a woman from the American West whose impoverished ancestors had come to the New World in order to survive.

Lee looked away, suffocated by this kind of proximity to a man who was off limits to her for more reasons than his engagement to Sophie.

Before long he'd treated them both to a feast of warm brioches, ham, hard-boiled eggs, fresh fruit, yogurt—literally anything she wanted. Despite the heavy tension in the room, food had never tasted so good. She ate everything.

His eyes glittered over the rim of his coffee cup as he watched her munch on a banana for dessert. No doubt about it. He was fattening her up for something that could put her friendship with Sophie in grave jeopardy.

Lee struggled to find interest in anything other than him. But it was impossible not to take the occasional glance. In a navy turtleneck, his coloring and rugged features made a devastating impact on her senses. If her heart would just behave long enough to let her see this through and get on the train, away from him...

"Another roll?"

She shook her head. "I couldn't. Thank you anyway."

"Then I suggest we go in the other room." After wiping his mouth with a napkin, he got to his feet and came around to help her.

"Sh-shouldn't we put things away first?" she stammered as she started to get up from the chair. The action inadvertently brought her cheek against his. When she jerked away from the contact, she lost her balance.

His quick reflexes saved her from falling, but in the process his strong arms went around her, bringing their faces within centimeters of each other. She never heard the answer to her question.

Suddenly their mouths and bodies were gravitating toward each other, seeming to possess a will all their own.

"Raoul—" She moaned his name, helpless to stop her response as he coaxed her lips apart and then began kissing her with a shocking hunger that matched her own. Long, drugging kisses that couldn't possibly be viewed as tentative or accidental.

Deep inside she'd been wanting this, and could no more call back her desire than she could stop breathing.

"Lee…I've needed to taste you like this since the first moment I saw you," he confessed on a groan before before reclaiming her lips.

Lost in sensual ecstasy, she gave herself up to Raoul, never wanting him to stop. As time passed, their kisses grew more passionate. Her craving for him was becoming insatiable.

Forgetting where it could lead, she clung to him, wanting fulfillment from this man more than she'd ever wanted anything in her life.

It wasn't until she felt her back against the kitchen wall that she remembered this was Sophie's betrothed who was kissing her into oblivion.

In eight weeks her best friend would be the woman who had the right to get tangled in his arms, delirious with longing.

In panic, Lee wrenched her mouth from his. "We can't do this!"

"We already are." His breath sounded ragged. "It's the reason you're here with me. Don't be afraid to admit it." He covered her face with kisses before burying his lips in her silvery-gold curls.

"I admit Sophie sent me here on a mission," she whispered in anguish. "If you'll let me go, I'll swear I'll tell you everything."

He eased away from her. The moment she was free, she ran out of the kitchen. He followed at a slower pace.

Now they stood in the living room facing each other like adversaries. Those incredible eyes had narrowed until she couldn't see the blue. He lounged against the built-in bookcase. It didn't seem possible that a minute ago they'd been so enthralled with each other they'd forgotten the world for a little while.

"Any time now you can begin telling me about this mission of yours."

It was maddening to her that he could sound so in control when she was a writhing mass of emotions.

She realized that what she was about to do would sever her relationship with Sophie for good. But she'd reached the point of no return. So had Raoul.

"The Princess doesn't want to marry you," Lee confessed in a quiet voice. She didn't dare tell him about Luciano. Sophie would have to do that herself when the time came.

He stared at her for an endless moment, yet his enigmatic expression gave away nothing of his thoughts.

"Why couldn't she have told me that herself instead of deputizing you to speak for her?"

Lee needed support and found the nearest chair. Her heart had started to run away with her and wouldn't slow down.

"She sent me to Zermatt for the express purpose of getting you to come on to me."

At those words Raoul moved closer. "For what end?"

"S-so I could report back to her parents that not only were you unfaithful during your engagement, you didn't care if the woman in question was Sophie's best friend.

She counted on my testimony to carry weight with her parents so they'd call off the wedding.''

Lines darkened his striking features. "It appears your loyalty to the Princess knows no bounds."

"This time it went too far. I'm deeply ashamed."

"You shouldn't be," he mused ironically. "Sophie knew exactly what she was doing when she sent you. I congratulate you on a very convincing performance. Incredible to think that what went on in the kitchen was playacting from start to finish."

Nervousness caused Lee to clasp and unclasp her hands. "I admit I got carried away in there. You're the first man I've been with s-since my fiancé was killed three years ago." She averted her eyes. "It felt good to be in a man's arms again. Obviously I'm more vulnerable than I realized."

Please God, let that be the truth. Otherwise I'm in over my head.

"Not so vulnerable that you didn't stop us in time," he said in a thick-toned voice. "I'm afraid if it had been left up to me we'd have graduated to the bedroom and wouldn't have surfaced until Roger demanded entrance."

Flame scorched her cheeks. He shouldn't have said that. It had started up a familiar ache that would never go away now.

"Raoul—" She tossed her head back to look at him. "Whether you believe me or not, I would never have gone to Sophie's parents to tell them anything."

His penetrating eyes searched her features, as if looking for something elusive. "Then why bother with any of it?"

"Because I didn't know I would back out of this impossible charade until…after," came her lame explanation.

Something flickered in the depths of his eyes. "After what?" he persisted.

Don't ask me anymore.

She took a deep breath. "After you opened the car door and discovered that Philippe had brought me from the station instead of Sophie. I knew then it wasn't going to work."

"I must confess you came as a surprise."

"Yes, well, the whole idea was ludicrous. Sophie should never have asked me to do it, and I should have had the courage to tell her no."

"Why didn't you?" he asked in a husky tone.

With adrenaline surging through her body, Lee couldn't remain seated. What she had to tell him was hard to talk about, but it was probably the only way he would understand her bond with Sophie.

"My father was a colonel in the Army. When I turned seventeen, he was assigned to the Middle East. Mother and I left Jackson to join him. Unfortunately there were no good schools for me there, so they investigated other avenues. Someone recommended Beau Lac and the arrangements were made. Sophie and I hit it off from the first day and grew close, like sisters."

She paused to catch her breath. "Three years ago Mom and Dad were living in the Middle East. I'd just been to visit them and my fiancé, who was also in the military. He happened to be my dad's driver. Sophie had come to Beau Lac to welcome me back. We were in the salon when a military man arrived to inform me that my parents and fiancé had been killed in a terrorist raid."

"*Mon Dieu*—"

She looked up at Raoul, fighting more tears. "There are no words to describe how I felt."

He folded his arms across his chest. "I can't imagine the horror of it."

"If Sophie hadn't been there for me, in all the ways of a true friend, I'm not sure what I would have done. Between her and her parents they saved my life, and have been like family to me ever since. The thing is, Sophie can be wilful, but when it comes to her betrothal to you I can understand why she has rebelled against marrying a man her parents picked out for her from birth, even if he is a prince.

"I-it's nothing personal," Lee hastened to assure him in a tremulous voice. "She doesn't know you. And you must admit that over the years you've shown absolutely no interest in her either. But of course maybe you were—*are* interested in her. If that's the case, she has no idea!" Lee hastened to add.

When he didn't say anything, she felt more confused than ever and rushed on. "I'm pretty sure she's lived in denial that the day would ever come when the two of you would actually have to do your duty. But her father didn't like the idea that she wasn't married yet, and I guess he talked with your father. So—when she asked me to do this favor for her, although I didn't like anything about it, I saw no way I could refuse her."

He nodded solemnly. "After what you've told me, I can understand that she put you in an impossible position."

Lee rubbed her arms nervously. "What's really ironic is that, after meeting you, I'm beginning to think that if the two of you hadn't been betrothed and could have met by chance, you might be looking forward to your wedding. Besides being attractive, you're both intelligent, wonderful people who are kind at heart."

"There's only one problem with that scenario." Raoul's voice grated. "Without the spark that drives a man and a woman into each other's arms, the rest isn't enough. Obviously you have already found that out."

Her chin lifted. "What do you mean?"

"You say you haven't been intimate with another man in three years. Judging by the behavior of my friends, who fell all over you vying for your attention, it's not for a lack of attractive, intelligent, kind, wonderful male admirers. But, as you've learned…if you don't feel the fire, the rest is meaningless.''

He was right… She was so on fire for him she knew in her heart there would never be another man for her. Her feelings for Todd were tame by comparison. That was what was so frightening to her now.

As she looked away, it suddenly dawned on her Raoul might have been telling her something else…

Sophie might have misread the whole situation.

Was it possible Raoul had never felt Sophie reach out to him in desire, so he'd withheld his true feelings? Had her rejection of him wounded more than his pride?

The Princess was a real royal beauty, who caused men's heads to turn every time she went out in public. Maybe all along Raoul had nursed a secret longing for her, yet had always sensed his betrothed's uninterest.

Heavens—it was entirely possible that he'd been hoping marriage would awaken her desire for him! It would explain why he'd allowed himself to become officially engaged a few months ago.

The more Lee thought about it, the more she wondered if Raoul hadn't wanted to take Sophie up on the mountain as an excuse to get close to her.

If that was the case, then how awful it must have been for him to find someone else besides his intended sitting in the car with Philippe!

A shudder passed through Lee's body when she realized what she'd said to him minutes ago.

The Princess doesn't want to marry you.

How cruel that must have sounded, especially if in the depths of his soul Raoul had been looking forward to his marriage.

This was agony in a new dimension. Not only for him, but for Lee, who couldn't imagine the bleakness of her life without him now. Their passionate interlude in the kitchen had probably been his way of venting his pain and frustration. But it had been a lifechanging experience for her.

She had to get away from him!

"I've been as honest with you as I know how to be. If you don't mind, I'd like to leave for the train station now."

He studied her for a moment through shuttered lids. "What will you tell Sophie?"

"Even if it costs me her friendship, I'll tell her the truth—that I couldn't go through with something that is strictly between the two of you and nobody else."

"And what will you tell her happened between you and me?" he drawled.

Was he afraid? He didn't have to be. Lee would go to her grave with their secret.

She faced him bravely for the last time. "Nothing happened between us, Your Highness."

CHAPTER SIX

THE hell it hadn't!

"Since you've been so honest with me," Raoul muttered, "the least I can do is handle the matter with Sophie in a way that won't jeopardize your relationship with her."

His comment caused the mask to slip from her face. It fascinated him the way her eyes darkened to purple. "Wh-what do you mean?"

Pleased to hear the uncertainty in her voice he said, "What do you think I mean?"

He watched her swallow hard. "I guess what I meant to say is, do you *have* to do anything? Can't we leave things alone?"

What was she frightened of? "I'm afraid that would be impossible now."

Her complexion lost some of its color. "Please don't say that—I'll just tell her that after you phoned her I lost my nerve and stayed at a bed and breakfast while you left on a climb with your friends. That way she'll never have to know about wha—about anything else..."

You mean like the way we were communicating a few minutes ago?

Raoul groaned, still shaken by what had just transpired. No matter what she'd said about her fiancé, Raoul could have sworn there had been no one else in that kitchen but the two of them.

Mon Dieu, the taste of her still clung to his lips. The fragrance of her hair and skin still enveloped him. It was all he could do not to reach for her and finish what they'd

56

started. Yet in his gut he knew it would never be enough. He'd want her over and over again. He wanted her now.

"Raoul— Please listen— Sophie will forgive me because she knew it was a foolish plan in the first place. I beg you not to do something that could hurt either of you or your families."

Her earnestness reached out to him like a tangible thing. What was really going on inside her?

"Were you lying about Sophie's feelings?" he demanded.

Her eyes filmed over. "How can you even ask me that question?"

"Then how can I *not* do something?" he reasoned, as calmly as he could. "You're her best friend, the woman who's been in Sophie's total confidence for years now. At great risk, you've just told me the Princess has no desire to be my wife."

He moved closer to her. "You think, after hearing that kind of news, I'm such a heartless swine I would condemn her to a loveless marriage?"

"No—of course I don't think that," she whispered. "But you're not ordinary people. You have your duty to remember, which makes everything much more complicated."

"More than even you can imagine," he agreed. "But if she was desperate enough to send you here, then desperate measures are called for."

She searched his eyes anxiously. "What desperate measures?"

"You're going to spend the rest of this weekend with me out in the open. We'll give the press the kind of copy they've been trying to get on me for years. I can guarantee that by Sunday night Sophie's parents will be calling my parents to demand an explanation. When that happens, all hell will break loose."

Lee stared at him in horror. "I couldn't do that to them."

He gritted his teeth. "You mean after going this far you refuse to do the one thing guaranteed to help Sophie escape? She'll thank you forever." Driving the point home, he said, "Your friend's plan wasn't foolish. Her only problem was she sent the wrong woman to get the job done."

"Wrong woman?" Lee cried out, as if stung by his remark.

He nodded. "You folded before you'd carried out your mission. My plan will ensure nothing goes wrong."

She paced the floor, then spun around. "Have you considered how your parents will feel?"

"Of course, but of necessity they can't be my first priority right now."

"But they should be!" she blurted heatedly. "A-and what about *you?*" The color had come back in her cheeks.

He'd been wondering when she'd get around to the personal.

"If you mean, how do I feel knowing my betrothed would do anything to avoid marrying me, then I'm surprised you would have to ask."

A sound of exasperation came out of her. "Your whole life has been aimed at marriage to Sophie. Aren't you even a little hurt by what you've learned, especially when you were officially engaged earlier in the year? I know I would be," she admitted in a quiet voice.

"Maybe my pride," he lied.

If she had any idea of the excitement he was feeling she would call him inhuman. But all she had to do was slide her hand over his heart, as she'd done in the kitchen, and she would feel it thudding with emotions he couldn't take the time to examine right now.

"What is it going to be, Mademoiselle Gresham? Do I take you to the train? Or are you willing to help me make your best friend's dreams come true?"

While he waited for her to make up her mind, he decided to add the qualifier.

"If you can't find it in you to help me, then I'll meet with Sophie's parents later today and tell them I don't want to marry their daughter."

Her eyes widened in disbelief. "You mustn't go to them!"

"Why not?"

"Because long ago Sophie told me her father would have to be the one to break your engagement, otherwise your title is in jeopardy."

"It's too late to worry about that now."

"You can't mean it!" She sounded frantic.

"Lee—without your intervention I would have exchanged vows with her, ignorant of her true feelings. We're talking about marriage for a lifetime. In our case, ignorance would not be bliss."

Another moan escaped her throat. "I wish to heaven I'd never come here."

"But you did come. If you agree to my plan, it's probable Sophie will get out of our betrothal gracefully, and I may yet live to retain what has been mine up to now."

"At what price? Even if everything works out, you'll have to live with a tarnished reputation, especially when the media finds out I'm Sophie's best friend." Her haunted eyes searched his. "I couldn't bear for you to have to live down a scandal like that."

With those words, he'd been given a glimpse into her soul. It humbled him.

"You'd have to be prepared to suffer the same fate."

"I'm a nobody from America. It doesn't matter about me. You're the Prince!"

"You think I give a damn about it when Sophie dreads the thought of marriage to me?" he demanded.

His question tore Lee apart. If he was in pain, he didn't let it show and was a master actor.

"No," she finally whispered, with tears in her voice, because in her mind's eye she could see Sophie running into Luciano's arms outside the station in Visp. The joy on their faces was something she would never forget.

But their happiness would come at great sacrifice to Raoul, who, at this moment, was showing more character and nobility than anyone would ever know, especially if he was grieving.

She ached with love for him.

"You th-think you can do this and still retain your title?"

"I don't honestly know. What I *can* tell you without equivocation is that without the right woman at my side it would all be meaningless anyway. Help me, Lee."

She struggled with an impossible decision. "I—I guess if there's no other way out—"

A minute must have gone by before he said, "Besides everything else, you're a courageous woman. No wonder the princess has clung to your friendship. She's very lucky you came into her life."

Lee raised her eyes to his. "Believe me, *I've* been the lucky one."

"I'd like to hear more about you two. Why don't you come in the kitchen and talk to me while I do the dishes?"

He was putting on such a brave front she had no choice but to go along with him, hoping to help him feel better. But of course that would be impossible.

"I'm embarrassed to say I forgot all about them. Let me help."

Together they made short work of them while she told him about some of her more outrageous escapades with Sophie at Beau Lac. His deep laughter was contagious.

How sad that Sophie would never see the Prince being

the man of the house, drying the dishes, emptying the wastebasket. How hard it was for Lee to hide her true feelings when these precious moments with him made her so happy.

For a little while she could pretend Roger's condo was *their* home, that Raoul was her husband. As a little girl, she'd often played house with her friends. Little had she dreamed that one day she'd grow up to play house with a real prince.

After they'd cleaned up the kitchen they went back to the living room, where he put the mountain-climbing video in the machine. While he sat in a side chair, Lee curled up on the end of the couch to watch.

For the next hour she sat enthralled as she watched Raoul and his friends make their ascent from the base camp to the summit. She couldn't contain her noisy exclamations of fear and excitement.

"You faced so many dangers it's a miracle any of you made it back. I could never do it."

"Are you the same woman who wanted to climb the Matterhorn?" he teased.

"Yes. I know my limitations. It's a shame my father isn't still alive. He would have loved talking to you about your experience. Everest was his dream. But when he was young and fit enough to make such a climb he had a family he didn't dare leave and a demanding military career."

Raoul shot her a penetrating glance. "If I'd had a wife and daughter who depended on me, I wouldn't have gone either."

He got up from the chair opposite her and turned off the machine. Eyeing her from a distance, he said, "What did you do for fun in Wyoming—besides climb with your father?"

"I rode horses in the summer, skied in the winter."

"Did your fiancé share those interests?"

His question surprised her, yet, oddly enough, she didn't mind talking about the past. She wondered when she'd stopped grieving.

"He might have done. Todd was from Laguna Beach, California, and loved to surf, but he had a dream to see the world. We met in the Middle East. He planned to make the army his career."

"What about his family? Are you still in touch with them?"

"Not as much as they'd like. In my darkest time, Sophie encouraged me to look forward, not back. I think she was right."

"The more I'm learning about the Princess, the more I want to help her get out of our engagement without any blame being attached to her."

Lee rose to her feet, loving him all the more for the selfless gesture he was about to make for Sophie.

"I still wish there were another way to do it that wouldn't harm *you*."

"In case you haven't noticed, I'm a big boy now and can take care of myself."

I've noticed.

"Shall we go? I'd like to drive back to the chalet. We'll pick up your things to return to the sporting goods store, then play tourist for the rest of the day. I'll be buying you some things—don't be alarmed," he cautioned when she would have protested. "This is for Sophie's sake. I already know from Philippe that you wouldn't allow me to pay for anything yesterday. But what we're about to do is strictly business. It will show the world I'm taking care of you."

Lee had no defense for that.

"I'm looking forward to it more than you know," he added with a half-smile that dissolved her bones. Then he opened the front door for her.

She made the mistake of glancing at him, and felt herself falling into those fjord-blue eyes.

"Do you realize this will be the first time in my life I couldn't care less how many photographers follow us around?"

Lee knew those weren't idle words. The journalists were the bane of Sophie's existence. For Raoul, that aspect of his royal life had to be a nightmare.

Too soon Lee's picture was going to be linked with his. She shuddered to think how the news would affect both sets of parents.

After he'd helped her with her jacket, his hands lingered on her shoulders. "It's going to be all right." He read her mind with uncanny perception. "I'll protect you. You won't have to say a word."

CHAPTER SEVEN

"*BONJOUR*, Greta."

"*Bonjour*," the housekeeper replied, then stopped her sweeping to look up. When she saw the two of them in the kitchen doorway, her blue eyes rounded in surprise.

"Mademoiselle! I just read the note you left me." Her gaze darted to Raoul. "I thought you went climbing. What is going on?"

Already Greta could sense something different in the air. This was only the beginning. He could feel Lee tremble, but he wasn't about to let her out of their bargain now.

"We decided we'd rather spend the time in town than up on the mountain."

Greta's gaze grew more guarded as it swerved to Lee. "You must be feeling much better."

Raoul chuckled inwardly to see the housekeeper he'd known for years behave like a mother hen watching out for her royal chick. "It was your tea that did it," he interjected. "She'll be staying with me through the weekend."

While Greta mulled over that unexpected bit of information with disapproval, he turned to Lee. "Go ahead and freshen up in the bedroom. I'll meet you here in half an hour."

"All right."

As soon as she hurried away, he gave Greta his attention once more. "We'll be eating out tonight and tomorrow night. You and Franz are welcome to take both evenings off if you'd like."

She looked shocked. "What about the Princess?"

64

"You needn't worry about her. She's not coming. I'll be in the loft if you need me."

He bounded up the back stairs three at a time and pulled out his cellphone. The note with Sophie's number was still on the end table. After punching the digits, he sank down on the bed and waited for her to answer.

"Allo?"

"Bonjour, Sophie. C'est Raoul."

The soft gasp spoke volumes. "Raoul—"

"How are you feeling today?"

"Not very well."

"I'm sorry. Perhaps what I have to say will improve your spirits."

After a hesitation, "What do you mean?"

"I've spent time with Lee. She broke down and told me everything."

"I—I don't think I understand." There was a distinct tremor in her voice.

"You're an intelligent woman. I think you do."

A long, telling silence ensued.

"Please don't be angry with her, Raoul. She was only doing what Luciano and I asked her to do."

Luciano.

Raoul relaxed, falling back on the pillow in complete joy. So that was what Lee had been hiding from him. She'd been afraid to tell him there was another man in Sophie's life. *Dieu merci.* He couldn't help but admire her more for her caring, and her discretion.

"If you and I handle this right, there's no reason why you and Luciano can't be married before too much longer."

Sophie let out a cry of happiness. Then he heard muffled sounds which meant she was informing her lover.

"Raoul?" She came back on the line. "You're not furious with me?"

"Far from it."

"Truly? I pray this means you're interested in someone else too."

"Yes." Most definitely yes.

"But this is *fantastique*!"

"We have Lee to thank for everything."

"I know. I admit I used her shamefully, but I felt so trapped and knew you must feel that way too. Lee didn't want to do it. It doesn't surprise me she couldn't go through with the plan."

"You're lucky to have such a devoted friend."

"She's extraordinary."

His eyes closed tightly. "I agree. Don't worry about anything. I'll accompany Lee back to Nyon. By Monday I would expect your parents to have called off our wedding. Enjoy your weekend. *Á bientôt,* Sophie."

"Wait, Raoul! How is that going to happen now?"

"Read tomorrow's headlines and you'll find out. *Ciao.*"

"Wait! Raoul—"

He hung up, then looked in the directory for the number of the Alex Grill and made the call. Journalists lurked in the hotel foyer waiting for celebrities to pass through.

When Reception answered, he made reservations at eight for His Royal Highness Prince Raoul Mertier Bergeret D'Arillac and guest. Would they please put the best champagne in the house on ice?

Within five minutes the word would be out that he was dining in the village. Fortunately Lee had been around Sophie long enough not to be unnerved by reporters. At least he hoped she wouldn't be too dismayed by the barrage of questions and camera flashes. Tonight he was pulling out all the stops, something he'd never done in his life.

He turned off his cellphone and reached for the house phone. It took a minute before Lee picked up.

"Hello?" She sounded out of breath. No doubt she'd been in the shower.

"Lee—what are you wearing to town?"

He heard her hesitate. "I only brought two outfits with me so I don't have much of a choice. It's either what I had on this morning, or the black sweater and trousers I arrived in yesterday."

"Would you wear the latter? I have a reason for asking."

"All right," she said in a subdued voice.

"Are you about ready?"

"Yes."

"Good. I'll see you downstairs in a few minutes."

As soon as she'd hung up, he phoned the kitchen. "Greta? Do you know where you put my mother's black cable knit cardigan with the gold family coat of arms emblazoned on the breast pocket? She left it here on her last visit."

His father had had it made for his mother, but she'd never worn it in public because she'd felt the crest made it too ostentatious. With Lee's gossamer hair, she would look stunning in it while they walked around town.

"Yes," the older woman said tentatively. "It's in the storage closet near the base of the back staircase."

"Merci."

Raoul cast off his turtleneck and walked over to the closet to slip on a white fleece pullover. It was the only article of sportswear he owned that had the initials of His Royal Highness monogrammed near the right shoulder. He'd worn it once for an official family photograph.

He tucked the hem into the waistband of his jeans. When he'd pocketed his phone and wallet, he hurried down the stairs, eager to join the woman who'd transformed his life in the last twenty hours.

The woman in the mirror staring back at Lee had the same face as always, but she was a different person inside. In a few minutes her whole life would change when she stepped out of the chalet as Raoul's girlfriend. Once the news broke, she'd be labeled *that* woman.

For Sophie and Luciano's sake, Lee could handle it. By next week she'd be in Jackson, far away from any gossip that could hurt her. But she had a pit in her stomach over Raoul, who would have to bear the brunt of disgrace with no place to run.

No matter how he'd brushed off her concerns, he risked ruining his own life and everything his family stood for. Lee loved him too much to let him throw ev—

"Lee?" The rap on the bedroom door startled her. "I've put the gear we're going to return in the car. Are you ready?"

Help me, her heart cried.

She walked over to the door and opened it. Her breath caught. The elegant white pullover that could only belong to Raoul with those royal initials provided the perfect foil for his brilliant blue eyes. Combined with his striking features and stature, he looked every inch the prince he was.

"Would you come in for a minute and shut the door?"

He scrutinized her thoroughly before moving inside, nudging the door closed with his boot. "What's wrong?"

"I know we talked everything over, but we can't go through with this. Look—I'm not backing out because of me. I already agreed to help. But—"

"Then there's no problem," he muttered in a forbidding voice she didn't recognize.

"I'm afraid for *you*, Raoul. I've lived in Switzerland long enough to know you're loved and revered by the people. There has to be another way to do this. Why don't you and Sophie meet and discuss everything? You could call your parents together and plead with them to consider another solution so no one gets hurt."

His handsome features hardened. "You don't understand. Even if Sophie's parents wanted to let her marry

Luciano, royal protocol wouldn't allow them to dissolve our engagement without clear justification.''

Lee was so shocked to hear him mention Luciano's name she barely assimilated the rest.

"You *know* about him?"

"I just got off the phone with the Princess."

She shook her head. "That means you've told her what you're going to do, and she's still willing to let you destroy your life for *her*?" Lee cried out, aghast.

Sophie's revelation about Luciano must have devastated Raoul. He had to be in terrible pain right now.

"She realizes it's the only way out for both of us," he said in his deep voice.

"I can't believe it." Lee's eyes implored him. "Raoul—your life will never be the same again. This is all my fault!" Her eyes glistened over. "Oh, why did I ever come to Zermatt?"

"Thank God you did," he said emotionally. "As I told you at Roger's, Sophie knew what she was doing." His eyes seemed to pierce her soul. "If you'd been on the phone and had heard her cry of happiness as she told Luciano the good news, you would know I can't disappoint her now."

It was too much. She looked away from him. "If you're this determined to do this there must be another woman you could find to help you."

"I know several from the past who would pretend to be my latest lover without giving it a second thought."

He'd had other lovers. Of course he had. There was probably someone here in Zermatt who'd expected to be with him this weekend! Why did it hurt so much?

"But, as Sophie's best friend, you're the only woman on the planet her parents will take seriously. They'll know you and I had special access to each other through their daughter, and will assume we've been meeting secretly."

She shuddered. "That's horrible."

"It has to be horrible to give her father a reason to sever all ties with me."

"He'll denounce you!" she almost shouted. "You really think you can live with that when all of it's untrue?"

"We both want Sophie to be happy, otherwise you would never have come to Zermatt in the first place."

Lee couldn't argue with those facts.

"But it's so unfair!" she groaned the words.

"Life's unfair, as you've found out." He grasped her hands and held them against his chest. "Look at me," he whispered.

Slowly she raised her eyes to his.

"I need you, Lee."

She tried not to be affected by his words, but it was impossible when she could feel his whole being calling out to her. She'd been the messenger, now she had to finish playing the part to the bitter end.

"If you're sure," she whispered back.

His eyes darkened. "I've never been so certain of anything in my life."

CHAPTER EIGHT

"WHAT can I show you, Your Highness?"

The attractive saleswoman in the boutique could scarcely contain her excitement. The same thing happened no matter where Raoul took Lee. Everyone recognized the Prince, but it was the female population that went crazy over him.

Lee had thought the attention bad enough when she'd gone out in public with Sophie, but nothing could compare to this. Journalists and tourists alike hounded him along the street, yet he took it all in stride and was cordial. At the hotel, where they ate a *raclette* lunch, people applauded as he escorted Lee out to the terrace.

"We've been to half a dozen shops, but none of them had a dress to match her eyes." His gaze fastened on Lee. "They're lavender or violet, depending on the light."

The clerk had been concentrating so hard on Raoul it took her a minute before she realized she was supposed to be looking at Lee. After his personal observation, Lee felt equally dazed. Her legs were about as substantial as mush.

"We *do* have a dress. It just came in. Follow me."

When they reached the fitting room Lee noticed how the other woman kept staring at the black cardigan Raoul had thrown over her shoulders earlier to keep warm.

"I'll be right back, *mademoiselle*."

Left alone, Lee removed it before taking off her other clothes, wondering what was so fascinating. Raoul had muttered something about his mother accidentally leaving it behind after a visit. She gasped the second she realized the D'Arillac royal crest had been embroidered on the pocket.

Hundreds of people would have recognized it. To be wearing such a garment would show the world Raoul had put his personal claim on her. Short of kissing her in public, he couldn't have done anything that would have conveyed his disregard of his fiancée as completely.

Already there'd been a moment after lunch when he'd helped her up from the table and his lips had grazed her cheek. The contact had sent scorching heat to her face. The tabloids would love that kind of press. She could be thankful they hadn't caught a photo of him kissing her senseless in Roger's kitchen.

"Here we are, *mademoiselle*. I showed this dress to the Prince. He said it's perfect. In fact he would like to see you in it, and suggested these heels to match."

Lee took the articles from her. "Thank you. I won't need any help."

As soon as the other woman walked away, Lee put it on. The purple affair with spaghetti straps, an Italian creation in a soft crêpe de Chine, was stunning. The lines made the most of her figure without being immodest. But she couldn't face Raoul right now. There'd been too much intimacy already.

She dressed quickly in her other clothes and walked out to the counter. "It's all very lovely," she murmured, avoiding Raoul's eyes.

"You need hose, *mademoiselle*?"

"Yes, and a slip."

Before long she had her packages. Raoul ushered her out to the street amidst a barrage of camera flashes. Some reporter in the crowd called out, "Prince Raoul? Is the rumor true that you're not marrying Princess Sophie after all?"

Lee cringed, but he just smiled and waved before helping her into the car.

Once they were on their way, he glanced at her. "You couldn't have gotten much sleep last night. I have to assume that's the reason you wouldn't give me a preview in the shop, so let's get you home for a nap.''

''That sounds good.''

''I thought it would. You can sleep until seven-thirty. We have dinner reservations at the Alex at eight. Afterward, I'm planning to dance the night away with you.''

At the thought of being in his arms again she felt her heart take up a furious tattoo.

''Don't look so alarmed,'' he muttered. ''It's the thing to do at night in Zermatt.''

''I—I haven't danced in a long time.'' Her voice faltered.

''The place will be so packed all you'll have to do is hold on to me and I'll take care of the rest.''

That was what she was afraid of.

Six hours later, after a sumptuous dinner from the grill followed by champagne, Raoul guided her into a disco bar. It wasn't Lee's scene, but it was exactly the kind of place Sophie would have loved because the music 'rocked'.

Once again Lee heard whispers as people recognized Raoul. The manager was all smiles and arranged the best table for them, but her companion seemed totally oblivious. He relieved her of the chic white wool dress coat he'd bought for her while she'd been in the fitting room.

In the next instant he spirited her on to the floor, drawing her arms behind his neck before sliding his hands around her hips to rest against her back.

There wasn't a centimeter of air between them. Lee trembled so hard, he had to feel it. They might as well have been making love standing up.

''I told you there was nothing to this kind of dancing,'' he said in a husky tone. The warmth of his breath on her temple shot sparks of desire through her system, electrifying her.

"You warned me it would be crowded, but I didn't realize we wouldn't be able to breathe."

He chuckled softly. "That's the whole idea." His hands roved over her back where skin met skin. "Have I told you yet how sensational you look in this dress? I'm the envy of every man here."

Lee had been thinking the same thing about Raoul. He looked drop-dead gorgeous in his tux, a breed apart from any other man. The women in the room couldn't keep their eyes off him.

"Thank you for the compliment."

She lost track of time as one dance turned into another. It was the only legitimate excuse she had to cling to him. But as the night worn on she realized this was too dangerous a game to play. It was vital she put distance between them.

"Raoul?"

"Umm?"

"Do you think we could leave now?"

"You're not enjoying yourself?"

If only you knew.

"It's not that, but I couldn't sleep this afternoon and—"

"And now you're exhausted. That's fine. We'll go."

People made a path for him as he drew her through the crowd to the exit. Until more flashes went off, blinding her, she'd forgotten the *paparazzi*. They never let up, not even at two in the morning.

She was a throbbing mass of emotions on their drive back to the chalet. "Today has been like a page out of a fairy tale. I feel like Cinderella who got her dance with the Prince." She had to keep things on a light note or she might break down and tell him how she really felt.

"How have you liked your role so far?"

He was letting her know not to get too carried away.

"Knowing it's temporary, I'll be honest and tell Your

Highness that I've loved every second of it. But the thought of it being on a permanent basis is ludicrous. Your world and mine are so far apart as to be beyond comprehension.''

After the slightest hesitation she heard him say, ''Nevertheless the enchantment isn't over yet, and you still have both glass slippers.''

In other words, he intended for the public charade to go on through tomorrow night as well. But it wasn't necessary. She was convinced they'd given the reporters more than enough material for Sophie's family to call off the engagement. In one day Raoul had destroyed all the good he'd spent his life building.

As for Lee, any more time in his company would only bring about her final destruction. However, tonight was not the time to tell him she was through playing the role of his lover. Otherwise he'd insist on another one of his talks, where she always came out the loser. She couldn't risk that.

Still high on the feel of his arms around her, Lee's only salvation was to run inside when they arrived, and go to bed without stopping for a breath.

When they drew up behind the chalet, she saw another car parked there. Beyond it she spied Philippe, descending the outside staircase from the loft.

She heaved a sigh. ''I'm glad your friends are home safely.''

''Me too,'' Raoul murmured before levering himself from the car. As he came around to open her door she heard the two men greet each other.

Relieved because Raoul had been distracted for the moment, Lee nodded to Philippe, then slipped past them and darted into the house. She couldn't reach her bedroom fast enough.

CHAPTER NINE

RAOUL let out a groan as he watched Lee's whiteclad figure disappear in the darkness. This wasn't how he'd planned the night to end. Inside he rebelled against Philippe's timing until he saw the smile that lit up his friend's face.

With it came the dawning realization of what it meant. Raoul's heart did a violent kick. "The news is out?"

Philippe let go with a cry of excitement. "I not only heard it—I saw it with my own eyes on TV! It's the major story on every network! They all say the same thing. 'A beautiful blond American woman appears to have captured the heart of Prince Raoul. There's no official word yet, but it's rumored that he and Princess Sophie will not be getting married after all.'"

He clapped Raoul so hard on the shoulder he almost knocked him over. "When I think it was less than a week ago that I received a call from a man who sounded like he'd come to the end of his life. You're no longer that person."

They stared intently at each other in the moonlight. "No, I'm not."

"Have you told Lee know how you feel about her yet?"

"If you're talking physically, we almost lost it at Roger's condo."

"Things have progressed that far already?" Philippe asked incredulously.

Raoul nodded. "But the situation is complicated because I don't know if I'm fighting the ghost of her dead fiancé."

"Mon Dieu."

"He was killed three years ago. At the moment she believes she's doing all this for Sophie's happiness."

Philippe shook his head. "If ever two people looked like they were in love, it's you and Lee. After what I saw on television tonight, your broken engagement is a *fait accompli*. I'm beyond happy for you. But what about your title? Is it in the past now too, my friend?"

"I have no idea."

"It's not a small thing you've done." Philippe eyed him soulfully. "The main reason I came out here was to tell you your parents have been calling the chalet every half-hour since I arrived. Your father wants you to phone him no matter the hour. When I saw your cellphone on the dresser, I realized you'd left it home on purpose. He asked me to wait up for you."

"I'll call him." Suddenly Raoul clasped his arm. "Thank you for being my friend. Without your inspiration, I would never have thought to ask Sophie to join me here. It has set a process in motion. I don't know where it's going to lead, but it has already changed my life. For that you have my undying gratitude."

"You had mine when you saved me after that helicopter crash on the mountain years ago."

Raoul breathed in the crisp night air. It didn't matter what he had to face. After being with Lee, he had a sense of well-being nothing could diminish.

By tacit agreement they started walking toward the stairs. "How was the climb?"

"Good. Naturally it would have been better if you'd been along, but I'll forgive you this time."

A smile broke the corner of Raoul's mouth. "I didn't know I could feel like this."

"That's what I've been telling myself since I met Kellie," Philippe confessed.

"Then don't let her get away. Do whatever it is you have to do."

"I intend to."

After what had transpired here in Zermatt, Raoul realized anything was possible. Right now his whole purpose was to make Lee see that too. Physically and emotionally, they were attuned. It was her mind that had to get past the prince part to the man.

After what she'd told him on the drive home, that part wasn't going to be easy. She'd been around Sophie long enough to see past the trappings to the kind of life required of a royal. Obviously it held no appeal.

But he couldn't worry about that right now. At least when he woke up in the morning she'd be under the same roof and they'd spend another glorious day and night together.

He climbed the stairs after Philippe, aware the adrenaline surging through his body wouldn't allow him to fall asleep for hours.

Now was the time for the talk with his parents.

For the first time in his life, they weren't his first priority. He had to count on their understanding that what they'd seen and heard on the news tonight had happened for a specific reason. He prayed that because of the strong bond of love and trust that had always existed between the three of them they would reserve judgement until they'd heard from him.

He planned to tell them the truth of everything. Destiny would have to take care of the rest.

"Madame Simoness?"

The older woman looked up from her desk. "Lee— you're back a day early from Zermatt. I didn't expect you home until Sunday night. Come in."

"Thank you, *madame*."

Lee shut the office door and took a seat opposite the desk of the headmistress who'd always been so good to her. She was close to eighty, but *madame's* wise gray eyes still regarded her as shrewdly as ever.

"What's wrong, *ma chère*?"

"I'm sure you've heard the news by now."

"Yes. My phone hasn't stopped ringing."

"I knew that would be the case. *Madame?* I happen to know Mademoiselle Lambert would give anything to have my job. Would you consider letting her take my place until you find someone permanent?"

"Why would I do that?"

"I'm going back to America. There's an eleven a.m. flight to Brussels from Geneva this morning. I *have* to be on it."

"Lee—if you thought I would fire you over this, you're very much mistaken."

"No. You're too kind for that."

"Then it's true—"

"What do you mean?"

"You've fallen in love with Sophie's prince, haven't you?"

So many emotions had welled up inside Lee she couldn't stop the tears. They gushed down her face until she was convulsed.

"I—I'm sure you think I'm a wicked person."

"Nonsense. As soon as I read this morning's headlines I saw Sophie's hand somewhere in all this. Remember, I've known the two of you for a long time. She was always the one at the bottom of any trouble around here. The poor thing had too much to rebel against."

Madame Simoness understood a lot about life. That was what made her such a remarkable substitute mother for the girls at Beau Lac.

"Why don't you begin at the beginning and tell me everything?"

It felt so good to confide in someone Lee trusted, and it all came pouring out. Everything except for the interlude in Roger's kitchen.

"...so as soon as Raoul brought me home from the disco bar I realized I couldn't stay in Zermatt another second. I left the things he'd bought me on the bed. Then I packed my bag and walked down to the village station."

"In the dark?"

"Yes. I wanted to be on the first train back to Visp. From there I rented a car and drove straight here. It won't be long before he discovers I'm missing. *Madame*—I don't want him to find me. I've played the part he asked me to play. Now it's over. There are other titled women his family will suggest he marry in place of Sophie. At this point it will be much better for Raoul if I disappear. I'm so sorry to run out on you like this, but I can't stay here! I simply can't."

"Is this to be a permanent move on your part?"

"Yes."

"I see." After a brief silence, "Of course you're free to go. Whenever you wish."

"You mean it?" she cried out.

"*Bien sûr*. Even when you were mourning your family, you never let up in your duties. I worried about that. It wouldn't surprise me that it has all caught up with you. I'll phone Mademoiselle Lambert right now and ask her to come over."

Lee jumped up from the chair and rushed around to hug the older woman. "Thank you, *madame*. I'll never be able to repay you for everything."

"Nonsense. You've been through a life-changing experience far too early in your young life. I want you to find happiness, *ma chère*. I had hoped it would be here in Switzerland, but evidently that's not the case.

"If you're going to make that flight, you need to leave for Geneva in the next few minutes. On your way out, come back in here. There'll be a check for you on my desk."

"I don't deserve your kindness."

"Of course you do. You're the best assistant I ever had. Don't worry about your things. The maids can pack up your belongings and I'll have them shipped to your address in Jackson. It's still in my file."

"If you wouldn't mind, could you ask them to take them up to the attic? You see, my parents's house is being rented at the moment. Their things are in storage. I'll probably stay in Montana with my aunt and uncle until I'm free to move back to Jackson. Even then I may sell up and move somewhere else. When I'm settled in a place for good I'll send for my things here. Right now e-everything's so up in the air I can't make definite plans."

"Of course not. I'm just thankful you have relatives who love you and will be happy to see you. Promise me you'll stay in close touch?"

"I swear it." She sniffed. "*Madame?* There's one more thing. I've written Sophie a letter and put a stamp on it. Will you wait a week and then put it in the post?"

"Consider it done."

They embraced once more before she hurried from the office and raced up to her room on the third floor. All she needed to do was put a few more blouses, jeans and shorts in her suitcase. She wouldn't need anything else until she knew what she was going to do about the rest of her life.

For the moment nothing was as important as putting an ocean between her and Raoul.

Philippe finished off his croissant with another cup of tea. "You keep pacing the floor like that and you're going to wear a hole in it, *mon ami*. It's only nine-thirty. After a night of dancing, I wouldn't be surprised if she slept till noon.''

Raoul's frown turned into a grimace. He eyed his friend. ''I doubt she could sleep anymore than I could. I'm going to phone her.''

He walked across the kitchen to the house phone on the wall and rang the guest bedroom. After four rings he decided she could be in the shower. When he'd counted twenty of them, he knew something was wrong and hung up.

Filled with alarm, he left the kitchen and raced down the hall. ''Lee?'' he called out before opening her door.

His gaze fell on the purple dress and shoes laid out neatly on top of the made-up bed. Alongside them were the coat and his mother's sweater. He groaned as if someone had just planted a fist in his gut.

''She's gone!''

Philippe was right behind him. ''Maybe she went out the front door for a walk.''

''You don't believe that anymore than I do.''

''I'll contact the taxi service and find out when she left.''

While Philippe phoned from the bedside table, Raoul picked up one of the shoes she'd worn dancing. As he dangled it by its dainty strap, a certain conversation came back to him in full force.

I feel like Cinderella who got her dance with the Prince. Except that the enchantment isn't over yet.

Mon Dieu, how wrong could Raoul have been?

Philippe hung up the receiver. ''There's been no call made from the chalet.''

''She might have gotten a ride with Greta and Franz on their way to mass,'' Raoul theorized, but he didn't believe it.

''We didn't go this morning.''

At the sound of his housekeeper's voice, Raoul spun around.

"Franz isn't feeling well."

"I'm sorry to hear that. Greta? Do you know anything about Lee's disappearance?"

"Nothing." She turned and went back down the hall, mumbling.

"I'll phone Roger," Philippe volunteered. "Maybe she asked for his help."

"Thanks, but you'd be wasting your time. He would have let me know if she'd tried to use him. It's evident Lee sneaked out of here on foot. The question is, *when* did she go?"

"Probably while you were on the phone to your parents."

"I told them I was bringing her back to the château to meet them," Raoul muttered.

His mother and father had been more understanding than any son had a right to expect. Touched by Lee's allegiance to Sophie, and the tragedy that had befallen her family and fiancé, they had urged him to bring her home so they could get acquainted.

He checked his watch. "If she left that long ago she ought to be arriving at Beau Lac any time now."

"Then let's fly you to Nyon right away!"

"You're reading my mind."

Philippe pulled out his cellphone and punched some numbers. "I'll alert the guys to have the helicopter ready for us."

CHAPTER TEN

THE sight of the Tetons had thrilled Lee all her life. But as her rental car rounded a bend in the highway, and she glimpsed those glorious mountains tinted an orange-pink by the setting sun, they brought back such powerful memories of Raoul she was staggered by the pain.

Why did I come this way? She groaned.

During the last month and a half she'd been living in a kind of limbo with her mother's sister and family. Between their love and a busy schedule guaranteed to keep her distracted, she'd managed to keep her heartache simmering beneath the surface.

After this long, she'd actually thought she was doing better. But one glance at the Grand Teton, reminiscent of the Matterhorn knifing through the thin atmosphere, and her agony came rushing to the fore, raw and unbearable.

She could never live here! There was no way. Lee needed to move to a part of the country where there'd be no possible reminder of Raoul.

During her time with the family she'd talked to her aunt about moving to Sacramento, where there was an opening at a private college for a teacher with her foreign language skills and experience. Though she couldn't imagine ever being happy again, she had to make a new start somewhere.

After checking into the Mount Moran Inn in Jackson, Wyoming, Raoul got back in his rental car and followed directions to the Greshams's modest ranchstyle home a mile away. Thanks to Madame Simoness, he'd been given an address.

He got there in time to watch an elderly couple drive away from the empty house in a U-Haul truck. Over the last six weeks he'd badgered them for Lee's whereabouts. They'd insisted they didn't know anything about her. But during one of his many phone calls from the château Raoul had found out they'd be vacating the house on the twenty-eighth of August.

That was the news he'd been waiting for.

Knowing the date, he'd made arrangements to leave Switzerland for as long as it took to find Lee and take her back with him. Her disappearance had created a living nightmare for him.

If the headmistress of Beau Lac had been able to give Raoul even one clue where to look for Lee in Montana, he wouldn't have left a stone unturned tracking her down.

To compound his pain, Sophie and her parents had left Geneva that same weekend as Lee, to go to an undisclosed location. Sophie had remained incommunicado. The last he'd heard, she had married Luciano and had gone on an extended honeymoon.

Without her help, Raoul had been left with no choice but to wait for Lee to show up in Jackson. It had been agony, and it wasn't over yet.

He got out of the car and walked up to the front porch. There was no Realtor sign or ''For Rent'' card anywhere. No phone number he could call.

That familiar sinking pit in his stomach was growing. He descended the steps and explored around the back of the house. Beneath a hot noonday sun his gaze took in the property that held so much meaning for her. From tiny baby to a seventeen-year-old, this had been her world, where she'd known happiness with her family.

Mon Dieu— How long did she intend to torture both of them? He knew in his gut she was far from indifferent to him.

Where are you, Lee?

He checked his watch. Two detectives from a local PI firm he'd contacted would be meeting him here in a few minutes. He was having the house put under surveillance to make certain he didn't miss her.

She *had* to come back here sometime. Until then, he wasn't leaving town.

By the time Lee reached Jackson it was dusk. Every motel had a "No Vacancy" sign. As usual the town was filled with tourists taking advantage of the last weekend in August before school started.

Since she'd made reservations at the Mount Moran Inn from her aunt's house, it didn't matter when she checked in. While there was still some light, now would be a good time to drive by the house for one last look. She had no desire to go inside and dredge up childhood memories.

Tomorrow she'd ask her attorney to put the house on the market. Then she'd leave for California.

As she drove through Jackson she noted that it had grown some over the last few years. Maybe six or seven thousand people made up the town. But the street where she'd once lived hadn't changed.

The old ranch-style home came up on the left. She pulled into the driveway and sat there for a while.

Was there anything emptier than a house without people in it? Especially when you'd loved those people and knew you wouldn't see them till the next life?

Her emptiness grew as her thoughts flicked back to Switzerland and all that she'd left behind.

"Raoul—" His name burst out of her on a sob before they began in earnest. Great heaving sobs that shook her whole body. "Dear God, how am I going to make it through this life without you?"

She buried her face in her hands.

Eventually the tears subsided enough that she could start the car and go back to the inn.

After checking in at Reception, she took the card key and walked down the left hallway to room twenty-five.

"Lee?"

A masculine voice that sounded achingly familiar caused her to drop everything: the card, her purse, the overnight bag.

She spun around, wondering if she was hallucinating. But the second her gaze fused with those riveting blue eyes she couldn't doubt the incontrovertible proof of his presence.

It *was* Raoul. He was here in Jackson, not Zermatt or Neuchatel.

Shock made it difficult for her to think.

"H-how—?"

"I followed you from the house."

"I mean—"

"Madame Simoness."

"You were there?" Lee was so dazed nothing was coming out right. "She gave you my address?"

"Yes," he answered in a solemn voice. "I would have tapped on the car window, but I didn't want to frighten you."

Lee started to tremble. Had he heard her cry out his name?

"What are you doing here?"

"Isn't it obvious?"

She shook her head in disbelief. "But *why* have you come? Has something terrible happened?"

His handsome face darkened with lines. "Yes. It's something so serious we have to have a long, uninterrupted talk about it."

Lee swallowed hard.

"You're in pain."

"Yes. It has become unendurable." His voice grated.

"I was afraid of this. Oh, Raoul—" She moaned. "I warned you, but you wouldn't listen."

"You're right. As a result, the situation is more precarious than ever. You see, my wedding is still on."

"To Sophie?" she cried in astonishment. "Then she didn't marry Luciano! Thank heaven!"

A strange look crept over his striking features. "What are you saying?"

"You don't have to pretend with me, Raoul. I *know* that, given time, your marriage to her will work, and you'll be able to win her love. She won't be able to resist you—"

"I think we're talking at cross purposes." He broke in on her abruptly. Shadows darkened his eyes. "I need to speak to you, but I'd rather do it in private than out here in the hall."

"Yes. O-of course. Come in."

He plucked her things from the floor and opened the door for her.

Like before, her arm brushed against his chest on the way inside. But this time it was like fire devouring her flesh. Lee would go up in a lick of flame if he so much as touched her again.

She heard the door close behind her. The click reminded her they'd shut out the world. It was just the two of them.

Her heart turned over at the sight of his tall, whipcord-lean physique dressed in jeans and a T-shirt. He had a hungry look around his eyes and mouth. She thought he might have lost some weight, yet he was more appealing to her than ever. His searching gaze took in the knit top and shorts she was wearing.

"I'm glad you're sitting down."

His remark set off more alarm bells. "Don't keep me in suspense any longer," she begged.

"I don't intend to."

He closed the distance between them and hunkered down in front of her bare legs.

"What are you doing?" she whispered in an unsteady voice as one of his hands went to the calf of her right leg while the other removed the sandal off her foot.

His dark-blond head was lowered in concentration.

"Raoul?"

The feel of his hands created an erotic sensation that wound its way to the very core of her being.

"I wanted to see if this would fit." A flash of purple and gold caught her eye before she felt him slide the other shoe onto her foot. It was one of the dainty high heels that matched the dress she'd left behind.

"I told my parents I would marry the woman who'd worn this dancing with me, and no other."

Marry?

Her thoughts reeled.

Surely she hadn't heard him correctly.

His head came back up. She found herself staring into eyes that blazed blue fire. "You're that woman."

Lee sat very still. "This isn't a joking matter, Raoul. I— I know you're hurting. So am I. But I left all playacting behind me when I boarded the plane for the States."

"So did I," his deep voice grated. "Tell me why you're still hurting. Is it because of Todd?"

"Todd?" she cried out in surprise. "Heavens no! I can't imagine why you would bring his name up at all. It's *your* pain I'm worried about."

"I hope you mean that," he whispered rather emotionally, "because you're the only person who can take it away."

"But Sophie—"

"What about her? She's on her honeymoon with Luciano."

"They're married?"

"Yes. Several weeks ago, as a matter of fact."

His slid his hands up her legs, as if he couldn't help himself. She almost fainted from the pleasure of it. Then he reached in his pocket and pulled something out. "I've come here so the real game of life can begin for us."

She gasped when she saw two different rings in his palm. He lifted one to her astonished gaze. It was a dazzling amethyst solitare.

"If you choose this ring you'll live in Jackson, Wyoming, with your husband and you'll be known as the wife of Mr Raoul Mertier. He's a banker and businessman with holdings in Europe and America which he intends to expand in order to take care of his family. He wants three or four children. They'll travel to Switzerland as often as they can to see their grandparents."

When Raoul pressed the ring in her palm, it began to sink in that he was proposing to her. If she was dreaming, she never wanted to wake up.

"I brought another ring. One I know you don't want, but it's important to me that I tell you about it."

He lifted it so she could see the bejeweled royal crest. "If you were to choose this one, you'd be the wife of His Royal Highness Prince Raoul Mertier Bergeret D'Arillac. There would be certain public duties attached to being my consort. You'd have private duties as well." His eyes had kindled with desire. "You'd live in our own wing of the Château D'Arillac in Neuchatel. Any children born of this marriage would automatically be a prince or princess. They'd have constant access to their grandparents."

He folded that ring in her other palm.

"Weigh them both very carefully, because once a decision is made there's no going back."

"I—I can't make a decision!" she cried in pain. "You're a prince— You'd never be happy living here."

Before she could say anything else, he'd cupped her face

in his hands. "Without you, I'll never know another moment's happiness. I'm in love with *you*, Lee Gresham." His voice trembled. "That soul-deep, painful kind of love that won't ever go away. It happened so fast and hard I'm still reeling. You were there when it happened, so you can't possibly deny it. Tell me you love me," he begged. "I need to hear the words."

Joy had welled up inside of her until she thought she might expire from too much happiness.

"You *know* I love you," she cried from the depths of her soul. "I can't believe you love me back."

"*Mon amour*—" he cried, before their mouths met and clung with voracious hunger. He pulled her into his arms and then they were on the floor, bodies, legs and arms entangled. The rings tumbled on to the carpet.

Swallowed up in a state of europhia, Lee covered his face and hair with kisses. Again and again she found his mouth, relishing its taste and feel.

"I don't think you have any conception of how much I love you, Raoul. At my house tonight, I sat there sobbing because I didn't know how I was going to go on without you."

He lifted his head to look down at her. His fingers tangled in her silvery-gold curls. "I wanted to comfort you because I thought you were grief stricken that your parents weren't there anymore."

"Darling—you have to understand. I wasn't grieving for them. I've gotten past that stage. Of course I'll always miss them. They were wonderful. But it was *you* I was mourning." Hot tears trickled on to her temples.

"Lee," he whispered emotionally.

"I thought deep down you cared for Sophie, that she'd hurt you. I couldn't bear it."

"Let's get something clear. We never loved each other, and never made any pretense about it. When I invited her to Zermatt I did it hoping she'd be so turned off by me she'd do whatever it took to break our engagement.''

"What?"

"If you don't believe me, ask Philippe. It was his idea. You could have no idea of the feelings running through me when I saw you in the car instead of Sophie. Part of me was in agony, because it meant my plans had been dashed. But another part felt this compelling attraction to you that went more than skin deep. Within seconds I realized I couldn't let you go.''

"I didn't want to go.'' Tears glistened in her eyes. "My behavior was so shameful, but I couldn't seem to help myself.''

"Thank heaven for Philippe's inspiration. We owe him everything,'' he murmured huskily. "Do you have any idea how wonderful you are? How incredibly beautiful you are?''

"I could say the same thing about you. The memories of what we shared in Zermatt have been tearing me apart. I've relived every moment with you until I've made myself ill with longing.''

His powerful body trembled. "We've both been tortured,'' he admitted. "I almost ravished you in the bedroom of the chalet when I brought you the tea.''

"I wanted you to,'' she confessed honestly. "Believe me, it would have been mutual.'' She stared back at him. "I love you so much. Since I've been home, I've found out what it's like to ache for someone day and night.''

"I know the feeling,'' he ground out. "There were times whe—''

"Don't say it!'' She silenced the rest of his words with her mouth. "All these weeks I've been terrified your parents would have picked another woman with a title for you to marry. I'm still having trouble believing any of this is real.''

"Didn't I give you two rings to prove this is no dream?"

"Yes."

"I told my parents you're the princess of my heart. They know the truth of everything and are looking forward to meeting you as soon as possible."

Lee sat up in his arms. "They don't hate me?" Her voice quivered.

"When they found out you were willing to subject yourself to public ridicule for Sophie's sake, you won them over."

She had trouble swallowing. "Is the talk against you very bad, Raoul? A-are you a condemned man?"

"Far from it. If anything, my popularity has risen to new heights now that Sophie's surprise wedding to Luciano Bernaldi has already taken place." He smiled before kissing one corner of her mouth. "Right now they're in Greece. My palace sources tell me public sentiment is demanding to know the identity of my mystery lover. So what I think we'll do is fly home and get you acquainted with my family, so we can make wedding plans. The only thing they have to know is that you're going to be my wife. Without you, there is no life."

His voice rang with truth. She could no longer doubt the depth of his love. Flinging her arms around him, she burrowed her face against his neck. "I feel the same way. I love you, Raoul. I love you beyond comprehension."

"Thank God." His voice shook. After kissing her long and hard, he finally relinquished her mouth long enough to say, "Here. Madame Simoness had this couriered to the palace before I left Switzerland."

Lee examined the letter he extended. "This is Sophie's handwriting." She tore the envelope open and began reading aloud.

"'My beloved friend—I will keep the beautiful letter you sent me forever. If you're reading this, it means Raoul found you, and you've put the past away. I'm so happy for the two of you, and of course for me—'"

Both of them laughed at her unique brand of honesty.

"'I cry all the time. Luciano thinks there's something wrong with me. He just doesn't understand what it's like to be let out of the prison I've been in all my life. Only Raoul could possibly understand.'"

"She's right," he murmured into Lee's silky curls.

"'If you're surprised that I know everything, don't be. Madame Simoness is my friend too. Of course we both know she loves you best'." Lee shook her head. "That's not true! 'Because you *are* the best. Raoul already figured out you have all the qualities of a real princess. That's why he knew it was true love the moment he set eyes on you.'"

He kissed her neck. "It *was* true love," he whispered.

It was impossible to concentrate with Raoul's mouth doing the most marvelous things to her.

"'The only thing you lack is a title. That's because you were born on the wrong side of the Atlantic.'"

"Sophie!" Raoul's chuckling had turned to laughter.

"'I wasn't cut out to be his princess, but you are. It just goes to show you that, given time, *la crème* always rises to the top. Marry him and go live in his castle, the way you used to dream. You always wanted Raoul. Now he's yours with my blessing.'"

Lee blushed a deep scarlet and tried to hide the letter from him. But he pulled it away from her and finished reading it while he held her crushed in his arms.

"'You think I didn't know about your secret fantasies? *Ma chère*, you were transparent over that gorgeous man from day one. That's when the idea came to me to get the two of you together. But I had to bide my time until Daddy decided on a wedding date before I could put a plan into action. Raoul's invitation for me to join him in Zermatt couldn't have provided a more perfect set-up. I knew he'd get one glimpse of those pansy eyes and fall like an avalanche.

"'After you're married, the four of us will be able to get together whenever we want. But I have to tell you—I can't wait to see you riding in the carriage next to your prince after you come out of the cathedral. Luciano and I will be watching and waving. Blow us a kiss, chèrie. Madame Sophie Bernaldi. P.S. Mother and Father don't blame either one of you. They know two people can fall in love very innocently. In fact Mother said she wasn't the least bit surprised, since she's always been a little in love with Raoul herself. P.P.S. They love Luciano because he's been willing to take me on and still loves me.'"

Lee burrowed against Raoul, trying to hide her tears of happiness.

Raoul ran his hands through her silken curls. "It looks like Sophie's problem is contagious. But I have a remedy. Let's get out of here. My private jet is standing by at the airport. We'll have dinner on the plane and you can sleep all the way to Geneva. We need to be married to each other, mon amour. I don't want to waste anymore time."

"I don't either."

"Then that's all that matters."

She cherished those words, but in her soul she knew it wasn't all that mattered.

Lee had fallen in love with an extraordinary man who had a special destiny. While she'd been reading Sophie's letter it had come to her that it was her responsibility to see he fulfilled it.

"Darling," she murmured, "before we leave, there's something important I need you to do for me first."

He pressed a passionate kiss to her mouth. "Anything."

Lee reached around for the rings and handed them back to him. "Will you put the amethyst on this ring finger?" She lifted her right hand.

His hands trembled as he did her bidding.

"I'll wear this in remembrance of a prince who was willing to give up his kingdom for me. And now—" her voice caught "—if you'll put the other ring on this finger?" She held out her left hand.

His beautiful blue eyes looked dazed. Finally he slid it home.

"This ring I'll wear in remembrance of the man who's going to be my husband, the father of our children, the man I'll love and adore through eternity." Her eyes fused with his once more. "It will be my joy and privilege to come live with you in your kingdom. Sophie spoke the truth. You've been the prince of my heart for a very long time, Raoul. You always will be."

"*Lee—*"

He gathered her against him. For a long time they simply rocked back and forth. She felt the moisture on his cheeks with a sense of wonder.

It made her feel a special kinship with Luciano, who'd also dared to reach out for an impossible love. One day they would have to compare notes. But not now.

Now Lee had all she could handle while she held her destiny in her arms.

THE KING'S BRIDE
Lucy Gordon

Lucy Gordon cut her writing teeth on magazine journalism, interviewing many of the world's most interesting men, including Warren Beatty, Richard Chamberlain, Roger Moore, Sir Alec Guinness and Sir John Gielgud. She also camped out with lions in Africa, and had many other unusual experiences that have often provided the background for her books. She is married to a Venetian, whom she met while on holiday in Venice. They got engaged within two days.

You can visit her Web site at www.zyworld.com/LucyGordon

Two of her books have won the Romance Writers of America RITA® Award: *Song of the Lorelei* in 1990, and *His Brother's Child* in 1998 in the Best Traditional Romance category.

**Don't miss Lucy Gordon's next novel:
A CONVENIENT WEDDING
available in August 2002, Harlequin Romance® #3712**

CHAPTER ONE

A SILENCE fell over the packed room. Lizzie looked up quickly, eager to see the man she'd come to find.

His Majesty King Daniel, hereditary ruler of Voltavia, twenty-fifth of his line, thirty-five years old, monarch of his country for the last six months.

Since he'd arrived for his state visit London had been full of official pictures, so she'd thought she knew what he looked like. But while photographs had shown the proud carriage of his head and the stern authority of his lean face, there was no way they could convey the vividness of his features. Lizzie noticed his eyes in particular. They were dark, but with a brilliance that she'd seen only once before, in a picture of his grandfather.

He was tall but carried himself stiffly, and she guessed that a press conference, such as this, came hard to him. In Voltavia he was a monarch, with a good deal of power. He wouldn't take kindly to answering questions from journalists, and Lizzie knew he'd been persuaded to give this conference only for the sake of 'good international relations'.

Before his entrance they had all been warned—no personal questions, no reference to his late wife. No questions about his three children, none of whom had accompanied him to London.

Now he was here and every line of his body showed how ill at ease he felt. He took his seat behind a table on a platform, facing the crowd with a practised air of polite interest.

The questions flowed. They were largely routine and his answers were the same, giving nothing away—the friendship of their two countries—mutual interests, etc, etc. Somebody mentioned his grandfather, the late King Alphonse, whose death, six months earlier, had brought Daniel to the throne. Daniel made a short, restrained speech in praise of his grandfather, whose lasting legacy etc, etc.

In fact, as everyone knew, for the last ten years of his life Alphonse had lived in a twilight world, struck down by a massive stroke. At twenty-five Daniel had become regent, and king in all but name. But Alphonse was still associated with the great days of monarchy. His long reign had begun when kings had had real power, and his personal prestige had ensured that some of it clung to the throne, even as he lay dying.

As Daniel mouthed polite nothings Lizzie mentally compared his features with those of Alphonse, whose personally signed photograph hung on her wall at home. There was a close family resemblance, not only in the dominant nose and firm chin, but in the expression of the face: proud, closed, unyielding.

They'd said of Alphonse that he was the handsomest man of his generation, and had still been saying it when he was in his eighties. But they'd said, too, that he was the most puritanical. He could have had any number of liaisons, but he'd been a faithful husband for twenty years. After his wife had died, if he'd indulged himself he'd been so discreet that the world had never been quite sure.

Only one woman had aroused him to a public display of admiration, and that was the great musical comedy star, Lizzie Boothe. She'd visited Voltavia with her own company, and the King had attended her performances. Perhaps she'd also given performances in private. Nobody knew for certain, and the King's reputation for rigid respectability remained untouched.

Daniel was the image of his splendid grandfather in looks, and also in the pattern of his life. Married young to a suitable princess, he had been a devoted husband and father, and had led a discreet life since his wife's death, three years earlier.

At last the questions were over and everybody stood in line so that the King could meet them individually. Down the line he came, stopping for a few moments with each person, shaking hands, asking banal questions about things he couldn't possibly care about, and receiving banal answers with the appearance of polite interest. He must be bored out of his skull, Lizzie thought, but he kept going resolutely.

At last he reached her and stood, professional smile in place, while his aide announced, 'Miss Elizabeth Boothe.'

His pause was only a fraction of a second, his smile never wavered. But she was close enough to see his eyes and the slight shock in them. So the name was still remembered in Voltavia. That pleased her.

As he shook her hand the King glanced at the identity tag on her shoulder, bearing only her name. 'The others list also their publications,' he observed. 'I think you are not a journalist.'

'That's true, Your Majesty,' Lizzie said, smiling.

He did not release her hand. 'You are, perhaps, an actress?'

Any man, looking at her flamboyant beauty and glorious mane of red hair might be forgiven for thinking so.

'I'm not an actress,' she said, 'but my great-aunt was. She was called Lizzie Boothe, and had many admirers in your country.'

Again the slight shock in his eyes: surprise, she thought, that she'd dared to mention such a delicate subject.

'Indeed,' he said in a neutral voice, and prepared to pass on, but Lizzie spoke hurriedly. 'I'm a historian, Your Majesty. I'm writing a book about King Alphonse, and I hoped you would grant me an interview.'

She'd tightened her hand on his, detaining him against his will, an outrageous breach of protocol as his astonished look told her. Instead of backing off she held him a little longer, meeting his eyes. It was a risk, but she'd never been afraid of that. At his side his aide tensed, ready to force her to release him at a signal from him. But it didn't come, and gradually the amazement in his eyes gave way to something else. Interest? Curiosity? Lizzie's heart beat with excitement. She was almost there...

Then blankness came down over his eyes like a curtain, and he pulled his hand out of hers. 'You must forgive me,' he said stiffly. 'I do not give private interviews.'

A curt nod of his head, and he passed on.

It was over. They were all being shepherded out, politely but firmly. Annoyed with herself, Lizzie returned to the neat little London house she'd inherited five years ago from her actress great-aunt, Dame Elizabeth Boothe, as she'd been at the end of her life. The Dame, as everyone had called her, had lived surrounded by mementoes of her great days: gifts from admirers, theatre programmes, some of them fifty years old, and pictures of herself in glory.

Lizzie had loved the Dame. Now she kept the house much as it had been when she'd inherited it.

On one wall was a huge coloured photograph of the actress at the height of her beauty and fame. Next to it was a picture of her most notable admirer, King Alphonse, taken when he was nearly seventy, imposing, autocratic, but still astonishingly good-looking. Near the bottom was written, in the King's own hand, *In friendship and gratitude, Alphonse.*

Lizzie tossed her bag onto a chair and confronted Dame Elizabeth.

'I made a mess of it,' she told her. 'Nothing happened the way I meant it to, and I just antagonised him. You'd think I'd know better, wouldn't you? I am supposed to be a professional.'

The Dame's eyes were laughing, her head thrown back in an ecstasy of song, but Lizzie could read her thoughts.

'I know, I know! Dress the part. That's what you used to say. And I didn't. If I'd worn tweeds and horn-rimmed spectacles I suppose he'd have taken me seriously. But why shouldn't I dress as I like?'

Good question! If a historian was a modern young woman, five feet ten with ravishing red hair and a model figure, why shouldn't she wear skirts short enough to show off her silken legs, and suicidally high heels? Why shouldn't she make up to emphasise her large green eyes and wide mouth that seemed made for the pleasures of life, of which laughter was only one?

If there was an answer, it was because she was as serious about her work as her appearance, which was very serious indeed. And today she'd blown it.

'There was one moment when I thought I was winning,' she told the picture. 'He looked at me in such way that I thought—I was almost sure—but he just got away from me at the last minute. *You* wouldn't have let him get away, would you?' She sighed. 'And I won't get a second chance, either.'

But, against the odds, the second chance presented itself next morning in the shape of a gilt-edged card announcing that King Daniel was pleased to invite her to a ball at the Voltavian embassy that very evening. After a whoop of triumph she got down to the deadly earnest business of making an impact.

The evening dress she chose was black velvet and swept the floor, but there all semblance of decorum ended. It was cut to show off her shoulders and bosom. The neckline was within the bounds of propriety, but only just. The bodice clung, and fitted tightly all the way down to her small waist, before outlining the flare of her hips, the length of her thighs and then down to her ankles. It would have been impossible to walk in such a dress but for the slit at the rear, through which the vision of her stunning legs came and went.

It was a dress for a woman who wanted to be noticed and could *afford* to be noticed: not always the same thing, as the Dame had frequently observed in her most caustic voice.

Lizzie had booked the cab with time to spare. No matter what the function, the rule was that royalty arrived last. To be late was to be shut out.

To her relief she reached the embassy in good time, and was shown into the great ballroom that looked as though time had passed it by. Glittering chandeliers hung overhead, the mirrors were framed by gilt, and its glamour was the glamour of another age. At the far end was a dais with a throne. Over it hung the coat of arms of Voltavia, dominated by a snarling bear. For a thousand years the bear had been the country's symbol.

When every guest was in place, fanning themselves and desperate for a drink, the great doors at one end of the room swung open, and the King began the long walk to the throne at the far end.

Lizzie recalled the Dame describing a ball at the palace in Voltavia, with King Alphonse in full dress military uniform, glittering with gold braid. 'So splendid, my dear! So magnificent!' Kings didn't dress like that any more, which Lizzie thought a pity, but she ceased to regret it when she saw Daniel in white tie and tails, which seemed to emphasise his height and the breadth of his shoulders. On some men, anything was magnificent.

First there were the duty dances. The King took the floor with a succession of titled ladies—a member of the British royal family, the ambassador's wife, the wife of a prominent international banker. Lizzie guessed there were a lot to go before he reached her.

She wasn't short of partners, and Frederick, one of the king's aides, solicited her hand several times. He danced well and asked her many questions about herself. Acting on orders, she thought, and kept her answers light and un-revealing. If Daniel wanted to know about her, he could do his own asking.

Occasionally the dance brought them close, but he never looked in her direction. That might have been courtesy to his partner, but once, when he wasn't dancing, Lizzie glanced up to where he sat alone on the throne and found him watching her. After that she knew he was conscious of her even when he wasn't looking.

At last Frederick approached her again, not to dance this time but to give a correct little bow and ask, 'Would you like the honour of dancing with His Majesty?'

'Thank you. I would.'

She followed him to Daniel, who watched her approach. She sank into a curtsey, but unlike the other women, who lowered their heads, Lizzie curtseyed with her head up, eyes meeting his in direct challenge. He nodded slightly in her direction, before extending his arm. She took it and he led her onto the floor for the waltz.

He was a good dancer, every step correct, but his body was tense. By contrast, Lizzie danced like liquid, gliding this way and that in his arms.

'I'm glad you were able to accept at such short notice,' he said.

Lizzie made the appropriate speech about being honoured before saying, 'I wonder how Your Majesty knew where to send the invitation.'

'I had you investigated,' he informed her calmly, 'and discovered you to be a historian, as you said. I gather you've written many letters to the Information Office in Voltavia.'

'Yes, and I've got nowhere. They just brush me off. But I *am* serious.'

'So I understand. The list of your degrees and professorships is impressive—and alarming.'

'There's no need for Your Majesty to be alarmed,' she said demurely. 'I don't bite.'

'But you do pursue. When you contrived to get yourself a place at the press reception—oh, yes, I know that too—you were in pursuit, were you not?'

'That's right.'

'And I was the prey?'

'Naturally. I only pursue the big bears. They're the most rewarding.'

He looked down at her with a faint, curious smile. 'And do you think you'll find me ''rewarding''?'

'I'm not sure yet. It depends whether you give me what I want.'

'And is that how you judge men—by whether they give you what you want?'

Lizzie raised delicate eyebrows in well simulated surprise. 'But of course. What other yardstick is there?'

'Are you by any chance trying to flirt with me, Miss Boothe?'

'Certainly not,' she said, shocked. 'It would be improper for any woman to flirt with the King.'

'True.'

'It's for the King to flirt with her.'

Her demure tone took him off guard, and he frowned, as though unsure that he'd heard her correctly. Then he smiled, cautiously.

'And if the King didn't flirt with her?' he asked. 'Might she not show a little enterprise in the matter?'

'She wouldn't dare,' Lizzie informed him, straight-faced. 'Lest he think her impertinent.'

'I don't think you fear the opinion of any man, Miss Boothe.'

'But Your Majesty is a king, not a man.'

'Is that what you think?'

She looked straight into his face, saying demurely, 'I'm waiting for you to tell me what to think.'

'By heaven, you're a cool one!' he exclaimed softly.

'But of course. A woman would need to stay cool when entering the bear's cave,' she pointed out. 'Unless she's well protected.'

'You, I think, are protected by your effrontery.'

'Oh, dear! I have offended Your Majesty.'

His eyes gleamed. 'Do not fish for compliments, Miss Boothe.'

'Is that what I was doing?' she murmured.

'Yes. And it was quite unnecessary.'

There were a dozen ways to take that but, raising a questioning eyebrow to him, she sensed exactly what he was telling her and a swift excitement scurried through her veins.

She hadn't meant this to happen. So far and no further. That had been the idea. Flirt with him, intrigue him until he was putty in her hands. It had worked before.

'Use your charms to bring them to heel,' Dame Elizabeth had always advised. 'What else are charms *for*?'

But it had never been part of the plan for *him* to charm *her*. Now matters were getting out of hand. Beneath his stiff exterior this man had a devil in his eyes. Lizzie had an uneasy feeling that he'd sized her up and decided he could deal with her.

But how? That was the question that made her blood race. Whatever the answer she decided she was going to enjoy it, and if she could gain her professional goals as well, so much the better.

'The music is ending,' Daniel observed. 'But our talk is just beginning. I've ordered champagne served on the terrace.'

Two hundred pairs of eyes watched him lead her from the floor and through the French windows that led onto the broad terrace. A footman was just laying down a tray bearing two fluted glasses and a bottle. Daniel waved him away, indicated for Lizzie to sit at the small table, and himself did the pouring.

'So you're writing a book about my grandfather?' he said, putting the glass into her hand and seating himself opposite. Through the tall windows Lizzie could see couples swirling by as the dance resumed, and hear the soft swell of music. But she was intensely conscious of the King, watching her closely, as though she was the only person in the world. 'Why do you wish to do this?'

'Because he's fascinated me all my life,' she replied. 'Aunt Lizzie told me so much about him, and about Voltavia. She made it sound like a wonderful country.'

'It *is* a wonderful country. And I know she had many admirers there. Among whom, of course, was the King.'

'She always kept the medals and decorations he gave her. She was a compulsive hoarder. I don't think she ever threw anything away. When she died she left everything to me, and I still have them all—the medals, the scrapbooks, even some of her costumes.'

'You must have meant a great deal to her.'

'She was my grandfather's sister and almost the only family I had. When I was ten my parents died and she took me in. She was thought very scandalous when she was young, but when I knew her she'd become Dame Elizabeth Boothe, and very respectable.'

'And I suppose you were completely in her confidence?'

Lizzie considered. 'Not completely. I don't think she told everything to anyone. She lived in the public eye but she kept many secrets.'

'But some secrets are harder to keep than others.'

'If you mean the fact that King Alphonse admired her, no, that was hardly a secret, especially with all the jewellery he gave her.'

'He gave her jewels? I must admit I didn't know that.'

Lizzie touched the diamond necklace and matching earrings that blazed against her fair skin. 'These came from him.'

Daniel looked hard at the flashing gems. 'Magnificent,' he murmured. 'Clearly he valued her a great deal. But how did she value him?'

'She kept his photograph on her wall to the end of her life.' Daniel shrugged, and she said quickly, 'No, it wasn't just a formal picture. It was inscribed in his own handwriting.'

He was suddenly alert. 'What did he write?'

'"In friendship and gratitude, Alphonse,"' Lizzie replied.

'"Friendship and gratitude,"' Daniel repeated slowly. 'Yes, my grandfather was a restrained man. I can imagine him using such words when what he really meant was something else—something a great deal more intense and emotional.'

There was a new note in his voice as he said the last words that made the silence hang heavy between them. For a mad moment Lizzie wondered if she'd strayed into something that was too much for her. This man held every card in the pack, yet she was trying to gamble with him on equal terms. It was heady wine, and his sudden urgent tone made it headier still.

The music of the waltz was floating out onto the terrace.

'Dance with me,' he commanded, taking her into his arms without waiting for her answer.

In the ballroom he had danced correctly, preserving the proper distance of a few inches between them, and touching her back so lightly that she'd barely felt it. Now he held her close enough for her to feel his breath on her bare shoulder, and his hand was firm in the small of her back. She had said that he was only a king, not a man. And she'd been so wrong.

'What do they call you?' he murmured. 'Liz? Elizabeth?'

'Lizzie.'

'Lizzie, I'm glad we've had this talk. It makes many things clearer.'

'Do you mean that you'll help me?' she asked eagerly.

'Ah, yes, you want an interview.'

'And much, much more.'

There was a sudden keen look in his eyes. 'How much more?' he asked.

'Access to the royal archives,' she said, breathless with hope. 'Official memos, private correspondence...'

'Private—?' With a swift movement his hand tightened on her waist, drawing her hard against him.

'I want to show him in the round, and for that I must see everything,' she said, speaking breathlessly for he was holding her very tightly. 'We all know the face he presented to the world, but it's the things the world didn't know that have real value.'

'Ah, yes. Value. We mustn't forget that. And of course their value is higher precisely *because* the world doesn't know.'

'Exactly. There's no substitute for private letters.'

'I'm sure that's true,' he murmured, sending warm breath skittering across her cheek. She saw how very close his mouth was to her own, and tried to control her riotous thoughts. But they wouldn't be controlled. They raced ahead, speculating about the shape of his mouth, the firmness of his lips, how they would feel against hers...

She looked up and what she saw gave her a shock. Despite the apparent ardour in his behaviour there was only cool calculation in his eyes.

She tried to clear her head, to know what this meant, but that was hard when the world was spinning around her. As they slowed she realised that he had danced her right around the corner of the building. He was smiling at her, and she could believe, if she wanted to, that the chill look of a moment ago had been all her imagination.

'You're not the only historian who wants to write about my grandfather, Miss Boothe.'

'No, but I'm ahead of the pack,' she said simply.

'Are you?'

'Yes. Because of Aunt Lizzie, who knew him as nobody else did.'

'I wasn't forgetting that, nor that such knowledge is *valuable*.' He stressed the word in a way that fell oddly on her ear.

'Priceless,' she agreed.

'I'd hardly say priceless. Sooner or later most things have a price. The problem is agreeing on it.'

'I'm not sure that I understand Your Majesty.'

He smiled. 'I think you do. I think we understand each other very well, and have done from the beginning.'

The reserve had gone from his eyes, replaced by something that made her heart beat faster. Almost unconsciously she raised her face towards him as he lowered his mouth onto hers.

She was no green girl experiencing her first kiss, but it might almost have been the first from its effect on her. There'd been a time when a king had held his throne by being better, stronger, more skilled at everything than his subjects, and perhaps it was still partly true, for this king kissed like an expert, ardent, subtle, knowing how to seek out a woman's weakness. Lizzie had never been kissed like this before, not even by the eager young husband with whom she'd shared a few months of wild passion before parting in bitterness.

His mouth caressed hers with urgency. In repose his lips were firm almost to the point of hardness, but now their movements were teasing, driving her as though he was being harried by his own desire. She tried to master her own rising excitement, determined to stay in control, but he was equally determined to strip control away from her. And he was winning.

He kissed the soft skin beneath one ear and she gave a small gasp. She was so sensitive there that normally she tried never to let a man approach it, but he'd known her weakness by instinct and gone for it without mercy. He continued the subtle assault down her long neck while she trembled and clung to him.

When he raised his head she longed to pull it down to her again and tell him to continue what he'd begun. Instead she became hypnotised by his eyes, which were brooding over her as though he too was trying to comprehend her, and failing.

'You came here tonight for a purpose,' he murmured. 'Was this it?'

'I—don't know,' she said wildly. 'Perhaps—'

'Ah, yes, the letters. Words on paper between people who are dead and gone. But we are alive. No woman ever felt so alive in my arms as you.'

And no man had ever made her feel so vibrant with life. Her head was swimming.

A noise from nearby made him release her reluctantly.

'We must talk more—in Voltavia,' he said. 'I leave tomorrow. You will follow me next week.'

It was more than she'd hoped for but she couldn't help rebelling against this diktat. She wasn't one of his subjects.

'Will I indeed?' she asked.

'If you're serious about what you're after, yes. Be there on Wednesday. If not—'

'I'll be there,' she said quickly, fearful of seeing the prize snatched away. 'I promise.'

'Of course,' he said, amused. 'There was never any question of your refusing. No, don't be angry with me. I hold all the cards, and you know it.'

It would have been wonderful to take him down a peg, but she was too close to her dream to risk it. She took the arm he proffered and they walked sedately back along the terrace to the little table. Frederick was waiting for them, with the reminder of an ambassador's wife who must be honoured. Daniel inclined his head graciously to Lizzie.

'I shall be waiting,' he said softly. 'Don't disappoint me.'

He walked away, leaving her to return to the ballroom on Frederick's arm. She felt as though she was walking on air. The glittering professional prize had been held out to her. That, she told herself, was the reason for the swift beating of her heart. That, and no other reason.

But she was deceiving herself, and she knew it.

When the last guest had departed the King relaxed with a brandy and soda, indicating for Frederick, his most trusted aide, to join him.

'Did she say anything of importance to you?' Daniel asked.

'Not a thing, sir. She replied to all my questions but revealed nothing at all.'

'That's no more than I expected. This is an extremely clever lady, but I have her measure.' A wry smile broke over Daniel's face. 'She's going to be a pleasure to do battle with. You know the plan?'

'Yes, sir.' Frederick took a deep breath before venturing to say, 'You don't think that this way of doing things is a little—a little...?' His voice ran down as his nerve ran out.

Daniel took pity on him. 'Devious, unprincipled, cold-blooded?'

Frederick ran a finger around his collar. 'Those are Your Majesty's words.'

'Coward,' Daniel said without rancour. 'Yes, Frederick, I'm being all those things. But then, so is she. This is no ordinary lady. She's sharp, shrewd, and utterly unscrupulous. So the only way I can fight her is to be the same.'

CHAPTER TWO

'A WOMAN is never too old to be glamorous,' the Dame had been fond of declaring to her awe-struck young relative, and she had lived up to her philosophy to the end. Life with the great lady had been fun because she'd never been less than exotic.

But it was Bess who'd mothered the teenage Lizzie. Bess had been Dame Elizabeth's dresser when she trod the boards, and in old age she'd still been her all-purpose maid and companion. When Lizzie had returned from boarding school it had been Bess who'd made sure she was comfortable, checked what she liked to eat, put flowers in her room. When Lizzie had gone out on a date it had been Elizabeth who'd lectured her about 'man management', which had been fun, even though the advice was often out of date. But it was Bess who'd waited up to make sure she was home safely, and Bess in whom she'd confided.

One time the Dame's advice had been spot-on when she'd tried to warn Lizzie off Toby Wrenworth, a daredevil motorbike rider.

'That young man was made to be a lover, not a husband,' she'd declared in her booming voice. 'Don't confuse the two.'

'Auntie!' Lizzie had exclaimed, not sure whether to be amused or aghast. 'You're not actually advising me to—?'

'I'm advising you not to confuse the two,' the Dame had repeated firmly.

But the eighteen-year-old Lizzie had ignored the advice, and in due course she'd wished she'd heeded it. The Dame had glared all through their wedding, but when the inevitable divorce happened, two years later, she'd been a rock. If she hadn't overflowed with sympathy neither had she uttered reproaches.

'Stop crying and get yourself off to college,' she'd commanded. 'It's what you should have done before, instead of wasting time on a man who was all teeth and trousers.'

The robust approach had done Lizzie a world of good. For sympathy she'd turned to Bess, and they'd cried together.

Even as a teenager she'd been sensitive enough to feel sad for the maid who lived in her employer's shadow and had no life of her own, although she'd always seemed contented enough with her lot. Since the great lady's death Bess had lived in a retirement home. It was a comfortable, even luxurious place, with large gardens filled with flowers, and Bess seemed happy there.

Lizzie visited whenever she could, and made a point of going to see her friend before she left for Voltavia. Bess was old and frail, but her mind was clear, and her first words were eager. 'Tell me all about your lovers.'

'Lovers? Plural? You think I'm living a really exotic life, don't you?'

'I think you're a pretty girl, and a pretty girl should have lovers.'

'Well, I have a boyfriend or two.'

'Do they break your heart?'

'Do you *want* them to?' Lizzie asked with a chuckle.

'No, of course not. But I worry that it isn't possible. You've been rather *armoured* since Toby.'

'Good thing too.'

'No, my dear. A woman should stay open to love, no matter how much it hurts.'

'But I am. You should have seen me at the embassy ball. Flirting. And more.'

'That's different, and you know it. Throwing out lures, as we used to say, because you're hoping to catch a prize.'

'Yes, and I caught him too. Oh, Bess, he's eating out of my hand. I'm that close to those archives.'

'Yes, dear, but you're hiding—as always. Work is such a convenient excuse, isn't it?'

Bess's eyes saw too much, Lizzie thought. Abruptly she changed the subject.

'What I came to tell you is that I'm off to Voltavia tomorrow.'

Bess's old eyes sparkled. 'How lucky you are!' she exclaimed softly. 'It's such a wonderful country.'

'Of course, you went there with Auntie, didn't you?'

'That's right. If only you could have seen her. She was at the height of her beauty, and she made a kind of triumphal procession around the main cities, and then she performed for the court. She was guest of honour at a ball, and danced with the King.'

'Did you see him, Bess?'

'Oh, yes. I was there too, in a little ante-room, so that I could look after her when she needed to take the weight off her feet. What's King Daniel like? I've seen his pictures, but they make him look rather cold.'

'He does, just at first. But there's something about him that isn't cold at all. I'm sure of it.'

Bess nodded, smiling. 'Ah, yes. Something deep inside, and he won't let you reach it until he's ready. Just like his grandfather.'

'Did the Dame tell you that?' Lizzie asked with a chuckle.

For answer Bess laid a finger over her lips, with a look of mischief.

'Have a wonderful trip, Lizzie, dear. And come and see me when you get back.'

*   *   *

Voltavia lay in the very centre of Europe, with borders that touched France, Switzerland and Germany. It had a population of a million, four cities, one important river, three official languages—English, French and German—and one airport.

Lizzie emerged from Arrivals to be greeted by a driver in the palace uniform. He took charge of her bags and escorted her to a waiting limousine. When she was settled in the back he showed her the well-stocked bar, asked what she would like to drink, and poured her an orange juice.

'It's thirty miles to the palace,' he said, taking his place behind the wheel. 'I hope you enjoy the journey.'

The first part of the trip lay through some of the most magnificent rugged scenery Lizzie had ever seen. She watched, holding her breath, as mountains gave way to pine forests, where wild bears still roamed, and then to lakes, serene and impossibly blue under the summer sky. At last they neared Durmann, the capital, turning off just before the city to sweep down the long approach to the palace.

It was a grand structure, a quarter mile long and built from a honey-coloured stone that looked beautiful in the soft glow of the sunset. Two Z-shaped staircases adorned the front, on one of which a man was waiting to greet her. Lizzie recognised Frederick from the ball. Smiling, he explained that he would be her host until the King was free.

They embarked on what seemed like a long journey, down endless corridors, until at last they reached the apartment set aside for her use. It was a charming place, a bedroom, a living room and bathroom, with modern facilities, yet a touch of old-worlde grandeur. When Frederick had gone Lizzie stripped off for a shower and a change of clothes that left her feeling ready to tackle anything, even Daniel.

Especially Daniel. Wryly she made the admission to herself.

She wasn't only here as a historian seeking facts. She was here as a woman who'd been passionately kissed and wasn't prepared to let it go at that. She considered the elegant trouser suit she'd just put on, and was dissatisfied with it. The green silk dress would be better. It took a moment to change and brush out her red hair again. Dame Elizabeth would have been proud of her.

And so, perhaps, would Bess. 'Be open to love,' she'd said, and the soft pounding of Lizzie's heart was warning her that suddenly she wasn't as armoured as usual.

The knock on the door brought a smile to her lips. Daniel at last.

But it wasn't Daniel.

'Your supper,' Frederick said, ushering in a footman with a trolley.

Supper was delicious, a wide selection of dishes, all perfectly prepared, and a bottle of excellent wine. Frederick was charming company, but he wasn't Daniel.

'I expect you want to go to bed now,' he said at last, rising. 'I'm sorry His Majesty couldn't see you today, but I'm sure it'll be early tomorrow.'

They bade each other a civil goodnight and he departed, leaving Lizzie feeling very cross indeed. She reminded herself that Daniel hadn't specified a time. She couldn't really complain. It was just...

She sighed. It was just that if he'd been half as eager to see her as she was to see him he would have rushed to her.

She watched satellite television for an hour, but took nothing in. She went to stand on her balcony overlooking the front of the palace, where floodlights picked out the two staircases and highlighted the building's elegant, symmetrical beauty. From somewhere above her head a clock chimed midnight. She returned indoors and closed the windows.

He wasn't coming now. She took another shower and

put on a soft peach silk nightdress before climbing into the vast antique bed that looked big enough for ten. It had probably been built for an orgy, she thought despondently. It certainly hadn't been intended for a solitary sleeper.

She wasn't sure when she fell asleep, or how much time passed, but it was very dark when she opened her eyes to the sound of somebody knocking on the outer door of her apartment. She whisked on the peach silk robe that matched her nightdress and hurried out of the bedroom to the main room. The soft tap on her front door came again, and she opened it cautiously.

The corridor outside was dimly lit, and empty except for one man.

'Good evening,' Daniel said with a smile. 'Forgive me for arriving at such an untimely hour, but I thought it best to be discreet.'

'Of course,' she agreed, backing away to let him in.

Daniel quietly closed the door behind him. Lizzie went to the main light switch, but he halted her with his hand on her wrist.

'I think not,' he said, switching on a very small table lamp. 'This will be sufficient.'

The tiny lamp gave a reasonable illumination, while still leaving the room half hidden in shadow. But she could discern enough of Daniel to feast her eyes. He was in day clothes, but without a jacket, his shirt open at the throat, looking more informal than she'd seen him before.

Lizzie felt at a slight disadvantage. She was sufficiently worldly wise to have realised that this moment would probably come. Even to hope for it. But had she hoped for it quite so soon?

Then she put her chin up. She was alone with the most dangerously attractive man she'd ever met, his dark eyes were regarding her with appreciation, and if she couldn't cope with that then it was time she retired from the fray and took up something easier, like taming lions.

'I'm sure you understand why I've come here so late, and so discretely,' he said, still with his eyes on her. 'In fact, I've been sure that we shared a perfect understanding from the first moment. Neither of us is exactly inexperienced in the ways of—shall we say—intrigue?'

She smiled, beginning to feel at ease. 'Does it matter what we call it?'

'Some people believe that to define things exactly is essential. Others feel that if the essence is right, the rest is froth. You clearly belong in the second group, which I must admit surprises me a little.'

'Oh? Why?'

'As a historian I should have thought you valued precise definition. And you are here as a historian, are you not?'

'In the presence of a king I am always a historian,' she riposted. 'Among other things.'

He laughed. 'Yes, let us not forget that I'm a king, because if I weren't you wouldn't be here.'

Not strictly true, she thought, looking at his throat and the few inches of chest she could see beneath it, rising and falling with some emotion that excited her. There was more excitement when he touched her face and wreathed his fingers in the hair that fell over her shoulders, drawing her swiftly close to cradle her head against his shoulder.

He covered her mouth swiftly and suddenly, kissing her with lips that demanded more than caressed. There was no tenderness, just an assertion of power, but while one part of her rebelled at this, another part, infuriatingly, was thrilled at the complete, unquestioning confidence of this man. His power came less from his rank than from his ability to drive a woman into a turmoil of dizzying sensation by his kiss alone. When he released her she was gasping, and shocked at how easily he could make her want to yield.

His face bore a look of resolution, as though he'd just come to a decision. Lizzie waited with pounding heart for what he would say next. But when the words came, they were the last she had expected.

'I think the time has come to drop all pretence between us,' he said in a voice that was curiously hard for a man in the throes of passion.

'I'm not sure I understand you.'

'I believe you do. When we spoke in London I had— shall we say certain suspicions? Which you obligingly confirmed. You've come here to sell, and I am prepared to buy.'

'Prepared—to buy?' Lizzie echoed slowly, trying to silence the monstrous thought that had reared up in her brain.

'At a sensible price, yes. You obviously know the value of what you bring to market—'

'And what *exactly* is it that you think I bring to market?' Lizzie asked, her eyes narrowing.

He looked surprised for a moment, but then shrugged. 'You're quite right to put negotiations on a businesslike footing. I'm prepared to be reasonable about money, even generous, but don't try to overcharge me—'

He got no further. What he might have said next was cut off by a stinging slap from a very angry woman. Then they were staring at each other, each trying to believe that it had happened.

Lizzie had never slapped a man's face before. She considered it undignified and violent. Now, in a turmoil of hurt pride, hurt feelings and sheer outrage, she was discovering how satisfying it could be.

'Have you any idea,' he said slowly, 'of the penalty for attacking the King?'

'Don't make me laugh!' she stormed, in the worst temper

of her life. 'All right, go on. Summon the guards and tell them that you tried to buy your way into my bed and got your face slapped. I don't think so. No man has ever had me for money, and no man ever will. King or no king! And if you thought I was for sale when you invited me here, boy, did you make a mistake!'

He was paler than she'd ever seen any man. Doubtless from the shock of being treated so disrespectfully, she thought with grim satisfaction.

'And I,' he said at last, 'have never needed to buy my way into a woman's bed. Nor am I interested in your charms.'

'That's a lie,' she said, casting caution to the winds.

He shrugged. 'Possibly. But I have never allowed my personal desires to interfere with politics, and you would do well to remember that in our dealings.'

'We're not going to have any more dealings,' she said breathlessly.

'That is for *me* to say. When we've discussed business I will inform you of our future dealings.'

'Why, you arrogant—'

'Of course I am. I'm a king; what did you expect?' His eyes gleamed at her. 'We're not just characters in books. There's still a reality behind the title, and the reality is power, especially here and now. I've wasted enough time. I want the letters.'

'Letters? What letters?'

'Oh, please! You know what you're here for.'

'I know what I'm not here for, and if you come any closer—'

His eyes flicked over her without interest. 'You flatter yourself—at least for the moment,' he said coldly. 'All that concerns me is the bundle of letters in your possession.'

'I don't know what you're talking about.'

He sighed. 'Very well, we must play the game out—

although I had credited you with more intelligence. When we were in London, you yourself told me of the relationship between your great-aunt and my grandfather.'

'Well yes, except that nobody really knew for certain—'

'*I* know for certain. They were lovers. Their correspondence leaves no doubt of the fact.'

The historian stirred in her. 'Correspondence?'

'When I assumed the throne I went through all my grandfather's possessions. Among them was a locked chest that turned out to contain a pile of letters. They were from an English woman who signed herself ''your own Liz, for ever''.'

'You mean they were love letters?'

'Yes, they were love letters, and they totally undermine my grandfather's reputation.'

'I don't understand.'

'He was known and respected as a rigid disciplinarian, a stern patriarch and an aloof monarch. Royalty, he believed, should ''keep a proper distance''. Because he lived up to his beliefs he was deeply respected, all over the world.'

'But he didn't ''keep a proper distance'' from this lady?'

'It would appear not. The letters are emotional and indiscreet, and they strongly suggest that his replies must have been the same.' Daniel's eyes narrowed. 'But I imagine you could tell me about that?'

'Me? Why should you think I know anything?'

'Because the replies are in your possession. You are Dame Elizabeth's heir, the one she trusted to preserve her legend. Who else?'

'But she never mentioned anything like this. And who's to say it was her? Did this woman ever sign her full name?'

'No, it was always ''Liz'', but she's the only possibility. The dates are very revealing. In August 1955 she wrote saying how much she had enjoyed seeing him again, and how sad she was to have left him. Dame Elizabeth was touring Voltavia in July 1955, and returned to England in the first week in August.'

'That certainly looks likely. But why did she never tell me?'

'If that's meant to be a negotiating ploy, let me warn you that it isn't a good one.'

'Look, I knew nothing about this.'

'Nonsense! You as good as admitted that you had them when we spoke in London.'

'I—?'

'All that talk about the value of personal letters. You stressed that your great-aunt knew King Alphonse *as nobody else did*, and that such knowledge was priceless. That was your exact word.'

'Yes, but I didn't mean—'

'And I, you may remember, said that sooner or later a price could always be agreed. You have my grandfather's letters and you've kept them to publish. It would be treasure-trove to a historian. But I don't mean to see my family secrets bandied about for the world to laugh at. You will hand them over to me. I'll pay a reasonable price, but I won't be trifled with.'

The truth was dawning on Lizzie. 'Is that the reason you brought me here—the only reason?' she demanded, aghast.

'What other reason could there be?'

She thought of his kiss, how giddy it had made her. And she'd rushed here, dreaming of more sweet delight. She could have screamed with vexation.

Instead she spoke with careful restraint. 'We seem to have misunderstood each other. I don't have your grandfather's letters. I don't even know that they exist. The Dame may have destroyed them. Have you thought of that?'

'Please!' he said dismissively. 'A woman? Destroy love letters? Is any woman discreet enough for that?'

'Is any *man*? Alphonse didn't destroy his, did he? I don't think you should get on your high horse about indiscretion.'

That annoyed him, she was glad to see. He flushed angrily and snapped, 'This argument gets us nowhere. I *know* you have these letters—'

'Rubbish! You know nothing of the kind!'

'Do not interrupt me. I know you have these letters because you virtually offered them to me in London.'

'I did not. I mentioned personal correspondence because that's what a historian always wants to see. I didn't know what you were reading into it.'

'You went out of your way to assure me that Dame Elizabeth kept *everything*.'

'But I didn't mean this. How could I when I knew nothing about it? If they were in the house I'd have found them.'

'A bank deposit box?'

'She'd have told me.'

They glared at each other in frustration.

'What are they like, these letters you found?' Lizzie asked, trying to sound casual.

'That doesn't concern you.'

'The hell it doesn't! You drag me out here under false pretences and *it doesn't concern me*? You'll find out whether it does or not.'

'If that's a threat, Miss Boothe, let me warn you, *don't*! People don't cross swords with me.'

'Time someone did! Frankly I wish I did have the letters you want, then I could enjoy telling you to whistle for them. As it is, I don't have them, don't know where they are, have never heard of them. Which rather takes the gilt off the gingerbread.'

His eyes were cold and narrow with displeasure, and if Lizzie had been easily afraid she would have started to quake now. But she was naturally impulsive, lost her temper, said too much, regretted it too late, and only realised the danger when it was long past. Daniel would have had to lock her in a dungeon before it dawned on Lizzie that just maybe she'd gone a little bit too far.

Possibly this occurred to him, because he relaxed and allowed his anger to fade into exasperation. 'There's nothing more to be gained tonight,' he growled. 'We'll talk tomorrow afternoon.'

'Unless I decide to leave before then,' she said with spirit.

'Well, if I find you gone I'll know what to think,' he said smoothly. 'Goodnight, Miss Boothe.'

She was facing a closed door.

'Tomorrow afternoon,' she breathed. 'Or tomorrow evening. Or the day after, if it suits you. Oh, no! I don't think so.'

Moving fast, she dressed, hurled some clothes into a bag and headed for the outer door. Opening it slowly, quietly, she prepared to step outside.

But, instead of the empty corridor she'd seen earlier, she now discovered two beefy guards standing across the doorway, firmly blocking her exit.

CHAPTER THREE

IT WAS hard for Lizzie to maintain her indignation when the sun rose on a scene of glorious summer. The beautifully manicured gardens were spread before her, trees, shrubs, flowers, winding paths, and in the distance a gleam of water. She had seldom known such a beautiful day, or such enchanting surroundings.

But she was annoyed. She must remember that.

She showered and changed into a cream linen trouser suit with a sleeveless green sweater. She finished off with a chain about her neck plus matching earrings. She was pleased with the effect. The chain was gold, but the bulky earrings had been bought cheaply from a market stall.

It occurred to her that she was all dressed up with nowhere to go, effectively a prisoner in this apartment until Daniel chose to let her out. But before her temper had a chance to get started there was a knock on the outer door.

'Come in,' she called.

Frederick appeared, leading a footman pushing a trolley on which food was piled.

'No,' Lizzie said firmly. 'I want to see the King, right now.'

'I'm afraid that won't be—' He got no further. Lizzie was out of the door and darting down the corridor.

She ran, expecting every moment to be stopped, but nobody tried. She had a reasonable idea which direction she wanted because Frederick had led her past Daniel's apartments the day before. After taking a couple of wrong turnings she found herself on the right corridor. At the far end was a large pair of oak doors with two guards standing outside. They moved together when they saw her, making it impossible for her to get between them, but she managed to knock loudly.

The door was answered by a man dressed in a neat grey suit. Everything else about him was grey also, including his demeanour.

'I would like to see the King,' Lizzie said as firmly as she could manage.

'Your name, please?'

'Elizabeth Boothe.'

The man looked puzzled. 'But His Majesty is on his way to see you. He left only a moment ago.'

'But Frederick said—never mind.'

She began to race back the way she'd come.

In her apartment Frederick closed the door of the cupboard he'd been exploring and said anxiously, 'I'm afraid I have found nothing.'

Daniel also closed a cupboard door. 'Nor I,' he said. 'But there hasn't been time to look everywhere. Still, I hardly expected an easy success. I doubt she's brought the letters with her; she's far too shrewd. Still, it was worth a try. Now more drastic methods will be needed.'

Frederick, a slightly puritanical young man, swallowed. 'I understand that it will be necessary for Your Majesty to make—amorous overtures to this young woman.'

An unreadable expression crossed Daniel's face, and he couldn't meet Frederick's eye. 'It would seem so,' he agreed. 'But for the sake of our country there are no lengths to which I will not go. *Ah, Miss Boothe!* How delightful to see you. But why did you hurry away so fast? Not reluctant to meet me, I hope?'

'On the contrary, I was determined to meet you,' Lizzie said, slightly breathless from running down the long corridor.

'But breakfast is for two,' Daniel said smoothly, indicating the table that had now been set up. 'Surely you realised I would be here? Frederick, you should have made the matter plain.'

Frederick murmured apologies and bowed himself out. Lizzie confronted Daniel, breathing fire.

'You actually dared to keep me prisoner!' she said. 'I don't care if you *are* a king, it was an outrageous thing to do.'

'You'll have to allow for the effects of my upbringing,' he said with a smile. 'It makes me tyrannical in small details.'

'*Small—?*'

'Let me pour you some orange juice. Strictly speaking, of course, you should be pouring for me, but as I don't want the jug hurled at my head I'll waive protocol this once.'

Lizzie was about to launch into her tirade again, but she found a glass pressed into her hand. She drank its contents and found them delicious.

'It was also a wasteful use of my men,' Daniel continued, seating himself and indicating for her to do the same.

'How do you mean?'

'Even without guards, you would never have left.'

'Oh, wouldn't I?'

'Of course not. Because while *you* may hold Alphonse's letters, *I* hold Liz's side of the correspondence. And you're too much of a historian to leave without trying to get a look at them.'

The truth of this struck her, making her fall briefly silent, although it was maddening to have to cede him a point.

'But I *don't* have Alphonse's letters,' she said at last. 'I told you that last night.'

'Ah, yes. A pity. We might have struck a deal.'

Lizzie's lips twitched. 'You mean, "I'll show you mine if you'll show me yours,"' she said.

'Something like that. But since you say you don't have them—'

'I don't. And the more I think of it the more I'm convinced that it can't be Auntie. She'd have told me.'

'Lizzie—'

'I think Miss Boothe is more proper, don't you?'

'Very well, Miss Boothe, the letters were written by your great-aunt. They contain details that leave no doubt.'

'But have you interpreted them correctly? If I could see what you have I might be able to point you in the right direction.'

His eyes gleamed. 'Very clever, Miss Boothe. You're a worthy opponent. Some coffee?'

'I'd rather have some letters.'

'So would I.'

'Then we seem to be at stalemate.'

'You persist in this pretence of ignorance?'

She was about to confirm this when it occurred to her that she wasn't being very wise. If Daniel really believed she didn't have what he wanted she could be headed for a swift exit, which no longer seemed so appealing. It might be better for her to string him along. 'Always keep them wondering' had been another of Dame Elizabeth's mottoes.

After all, she argued with her conscience, she'd already told him the truth. If he chose not to believe it, was that her fault?

'What is it?' he asked, studying her face. 'Are you about to come clean after all?'

She didn't answer directly. 'Your Majesty both over- and underestimates me,' she said demurely.

'I don't—quite—understand you.'

And I'm going to keep it that way, she thought. Aloud

she said, 'You credit me with more cunning than I possess, but less intelligence.'

Not a bad answer, she thought. It sounded clever, while meaning absolutely nothing. His eyes showed bafflement, as though he were seeking some deep significance in her words.

'I see,' he said at last.

You don't, she thought. *You're waving as you go down for the third time. Fine. You fooled me. Now we'll play my game.*

She spoke slowly, like someone still deciding her words, although her sharp mind was operating coolly now and her strategy was laid out.

'If you really do see,' she mused, 'then perhaps you also see that this isn't the time to talk. There are things to be considered.'

'I thought we'd already considered them. "I'll show you mine if you show me yours."'

'But yours is so much bigger than mine,' Lizzie pointed out.

'I beg your pardon!' He was startled.

'I don't just want to see letters. I wanted to browse through the archives. You have such huge archives, and I—' She shrugged self-deprecatingly.

'What you possess is valuable more for its content than its size—which, after all, isn't everything.'

'True. But don't forget I've told you that I don't have anything to trade.'

'That's true. You've *told* me.'

'But you have a good deal.'

'I am not showing you the letters.'

'I'd rather we left them for another time,' Lizzie said truthfully. 'Let's talk archives.'

'Very well,' he said, becoming businesslike. 'I'll send

my archivist, Hermann Feltz, to see you. You'll find him extremely helpful. We'll talk later. Good day.'

He was gone in a moment, evidently having decided to waste no more time on her.

After that the day improved. Hermann Feltz turned out to be a charming old gentleman, eager to be helpful. He took Lizzie to the great library and placed himself at her disposal. File after file was produced at her request. The historian in Lizzie took over and she became lost in her work. They ate lunch together, talking all the time, and Hermann told her what a pleasure it was to work with someone so knowledgeable and sympathetic.

Day became evening. The old man began to yawn and Lizzie said, 'I can manage, if you'll trust me here alone.'

'The King's orders are that you're to have everything you want,' he said.

She'd guessed it, and while it pleased her it also reminded her what a dangerous tightrope she was walking. When Daniel discovered the truth...

So what? She'd been honest from the outset. Was it her fault if he couldn't recognise the truth when he heard it?

She worked on. A meal appeared at her elbow. She thanked the footman who'd brought it and was buried in files again before he'd left the room. She spent the next hour with a morsel of food in one hand and a paper in the other, occasionally dropping the food to make a note. At last she yawned and stretched with her eyes closed. When she opened them Daniel was standing there.

'Still at work?' he asked.

'There's so much to get through, and it's all such good stuff,' she said happily. 'I can't tear myself away.'

'Don't worry, it will still be here tomorrow. It's time you stopped for the night.'

'Good heavens! After midnight. I lost track of time. It's fascinating, all those social reforms he promoted—'

'Social reforms?'

'Yes, I'm working on the fifties now. All those new laws—everyone thought the King was putting the brakes on, trying to maintain the status quo, but actually he was urging the Prime Minister on behind the scenes. He did so much good that he's never been given the credit for—'

'Or the blame if things had gone wrong,' Daniel observed. 'An appearance of political neutrality was useful to the King even then. But is that all you've been working on today? I thought you had other concerns.'

'Oh, his love life's interesting, of course,' Lizzie agreed in a faintly dismissive tone that she'd calculated to a nicety, 'but don't let's get it out of proportion. He was a fascinating man for many more reasons than that. I've been reading the cabinet papers for 1955, and guess what I found—here, look at this—'

He settled beside her and followed her pointing finger. 'That's misleading,' he said when she'd explained what had attracted her attention. 'My grandfather never meant it that way, but the Prime Minister explained it badly in cabinet, and once they'd seized the idea—'

He talked on, fetching more files for her. They argued. She talked about the lessons of history. He told her she didn't know any history worth knowing. He accused her of jumping to conclusions, she accused him of having a narrow point of view. Lizzie grew heated, hammering home her point with a fierce enthusiasm that he would have called unfeminine but for the burning, beautiful light in her eyes.

'No, listen,' she said, interrupting him with a lack of protocol that would have made his courtiers faint, 'you've got this wrong, and there's a document in the Public Records Office that proves it.'

'And what does a British office know about King Alphonse?'

'It's got all the cabinet records of that year, including his contacts with Sir Winston Churchill, and there's a memo that says—' She was away again, barely pausing for breath and not allowing him to get a word in edgeways for five minutes.

'Is it my turn now?' he asked at last.

'You're not listening to me.'

'I'm not doing anything else,' he said, exasperated to the point of raising his voice. 'Now, look, read this again—'

They were still at it, hammer and tongs when the clock struck two, amazing them both.

'Enough for tonight,' he said.

'Yes,' she agreed. She was standing, but she sat abruptly, yawning and running her hands through her hair, which had grown untidy.

Daniel regarded her, remembering the perfectly groomed woman of the ball. Now her face was bare of make-up, her eyes were drooping and she was too weary to be putting out her charms to seduce him. And that made her more mysteriously seductive than ever. As king, Daniel was used to women being consciously alluring for his benefit, their attractions all for show and not a thought in their heads but expensive gifts for themselves or advancement for their husbands. One who discarded politeness to argue with him for the sake of intellectual truth, and whose mental activity had tired her to the point of vulnerability, was new to him. She was suddenly far more intriguing than any woman in the world, and he had an urge to kiss her that was almost overwhelming.

Gently he took her hands and drew her to her feet. She opened her eyes and looked at him vaguely. 'Time to go to bed,' she sighed.

The words could have been provocative, but there was nothing teasing in the way they were said, and that provoked him more than anything. He fought his desire down. Not now, but later, when the time was right. And he would personally see to it that there *was* a right time. Whatever other disputes were between them it was growing clearer by the minute that she had to be his. He'd seen her as a woman of the world, boldly challenging him with her sexual promise. Tonight she'd been an academic, driven by an obsession with knowledge. Now the eyes that looked sleepily into his were as innocent as a child's. There had to be a way of reconciling those three aspects into the same woman.

Slipping an arm about her waist, he went to a concealed door that led into a bare wooden passage. It would take them directly to her room, and it was better that nobody saw them together like this.

At the door to her room he stopped and pushed her gently inside.

'Hey, I didn't know there was a secret passage here,' she said, waking up a little. 'Anyone could come in without my knowing.'

'Not if you slide the bolt across, like this,' he said, showing her a small gilt bolt that was almost hidden in the rest of the giltwork. 'There's another one at the bottom, and once they're shut you're completely safe from intruders.'

She didn't answer, only smiled at him in a way that threatened his good resolutions. He bid her a hurried goodnight, and quickly returned along the passage. As he went he heard the bolts slide across her door, and wondered if he'd just succumbed to a form of insanity. On the whole, he was inclined to believe that he had.

She breakfasted alone and went to the library as soon as she'd finished. Feltz wasn't there. Instead she found a boy of about twelve, who rose as soon as he saw her.

'Excuse me,' he said with a small bow. 'I was just leaving.'

He was so like Daniel that she had no trouble identifying him.

'You must be Prince Felix,' she said.

'Please, I am simply Felix,' he said, inclining his head again. He was like a little old man, she thought. It was charming, but it was also unnatural.

'I know who you are,' he went on. 'You are the lady everyone is talking about.'

'I didn't know that.'

'Only they do it very quietly. If anyone mentions you in front of my father he gets angry and tells them to be silent,' the child confided. 'But you won't tell him I said that?' he added quickly.

'Don't worry, I'll keep mum,' she promised.

He frowned. 'Mum?'

'It means keep quiet.'

He gave her a wide smile. 'Thank you. May I join you in here? I promise not to trouble you.'

'Of, course you can stay. But it's summer. Shouldn't you be outside? It's the school holiday. But I don't suppose you go to school.'

'Oh yes, I go to a school here in the city. But I have a holiday assignment to complete.'

'Don't you get any fun?'

'But of course.' He seemed mildly shocked. 'Each afternoon we go horse riding—'

'We?'

'My brother Sandor and my sister Elsa.'

'You go riding together every afternoon? Without fail?'

'Yes, and we enjoy it very much.'

'Yes, but—' To Lizzie it sounded regimented, however much they liked it, but she backed off from trying to explain to this grave child.

'Do you enjoy riding, Miss Boothe?'

'A lot.'

'I'll have the head groom find a suitable horse for you, and you can join us this afternoon. Goodbye until then.' Despite his youth the boy's manner was calmly authoritative, and she was reminded uncannily of Daniel. This child was like him in more than looks.

She worked until one o'clock, when lunch was brought to her. Afterwards a footman came to inform her that the Crown Prince was waiting for her, and led her to the stables. Felix was there, with a younger boy with a cherubic face and a girl of about ten with the beginnings of beauty. They greeted Lizzie politely, and the girl showed her some hard hats, inviting her to take her pick.

The mare they'd chosen for her was a delight, a docile creature with gentle eyes and a silken mouth. When Lizzie had spent a few moments getting introduced they were off, with a groom riding just behind.

The palace grounds were huge, with the neat gardens giving way to a park where the atmosphere was more relaxed. They gathered speed and galloped in the direction of the water. It turned out to be a lake, with a tiny pebble beach, where they dismounted to let the horses drink. The children took it in turns to ask her courteous questions, and soon Lizzie began to find their perfect behaviour slightly oppressive. To lighten the atmosphere, she said,

'I knew a lake like this when I was a child. It was in the local park and I used to compete with the boys in stone throwing. I could beat them too.'

'Stone throwing?' Felix echoed with a little frown.

'Like this.' She picked up a pebble, checked to see that there was no passing wildlife to be endangered, took careful aim, and sent the stone skimming across the surface of the water until it reached the other side.

'Try it,' she suggested.

Felix did so, but he couldn't manage the flick of the wrist that causing the skimming action. He threw 'straight' and the stone dropped into the water with a miserable 'plop'. Sandor had no better luck.

'Now you,' Lizzie said to Elsa.

'Me?'

'What they can do, you can do. And, if you're like me, you can probably do it better.'

And she did. With sharper eyes than her brothers Elsa had noticed the crucial wrist movement, and with her first throw she made the stone bounce along the surface of the water. Not far, but enough to goad her brothers out of their perfect behaviour, Lizzie was glad to notice.

Sandor was the next to get the idea. Of the three he seemed the most naturally aggressive. He threw and threw, his face creased into a scowl that threatened a temper if he wasn't acknowledged the winner. The gentle Felix did his best, but he was the first to stop when a duck suddenly appeared, followed by frantically paddling ducklings.

'Wait,' Lizzie said urgently. 'You might hurt one of them.'

'Let them get out of the way,' Sandor blustered.

'I said *wait*,' Lizzie insisted, taking firm hold of the hand he was raising.

Sandor threw her a black look but, reading the determination in her eyes, backed down. The other two children exchanged glances.

Lizzie had feared a tantrum from a child who was clearly used to getting his own way. But the next moment Sandor had shrugged the matter aside and was all smiles. He even began to clown, calling to the duck across the water,

'Excuse me, dear madam, would you mind hurrying, please?'

The mother duck cast him a startled look and began paddling faster, which made them all burst out laughing, Sandor loudest of all.

'Good afternoon.'

Nobody had known that Daniel was there, and at the sound of his voice they all swung around, their laughter fading to silence. Lizzie knew a stab of pity for him. It must be terrible for any man to know that his presence was a blight on his children.

And he did know. She could see it in his eyes, although his pleasant smile never wavered as they greeted him. He was their father, but first of all he was their king, and he was no more skilled than they at finding a way around that.

He asked about their ride and they responded with appropriate words. Lizzie did her best to help, praising the children as good hosts, he congratulated them, and they were all relieved when it was over.

The children continued their ride with the groom. Daniel looked at her, frowning.

'How did you contrive to meet my children?' he asked curtly. 'They can't tell you anything.'

Lizzie's eyes flashed. 'You've got a nerve, suggesting I wormed my way in. I didn't ''contrive'' anything. I don't stoop to those methods.'

'Then how did you meet them?'

'Felix was ahead of me in the library this morning. We introduced ourselves and he invited me to ride with them.'

He closed his eyes tiredly. 'Forgive me. I didn't mean to be rude. I'm afraid I grow suspicious of everything. Ride with me.'

She mounted the mare and the two horses began to walk side by side.

'Your children are charming,' she ventured.

'They are also afraid of me,' he said in a brooding voice.

'A little in awe, perhaps, but not afraid.'

'I haven't known what to say to them since their mother died.'

Lizzie could believe it all too easily. 'What was she like?' she asked gently.

'She was a wonderful mother,' Daniel said at once. 'She insisted on taking charge of the nursery herself. She left the nannies very little to do. She said that nobody must come between her and her children.'

Lizzie wondered if he knew what he was revealing. Daniel had nothing but good to say of his late wife, but through the words there appeared a picture of a woman who had not loved her husband and had consoled herself with her children. He gave no hint as to whether he had loved Serena, but it was clear that her remoteness had left him lonelier. The right woman could have drawn him out, she thought, encouraged the warmth that she was sure was there in him. If she'd loved him...

Lizzie pulled herself together, wondering where her wits were wandering. It was Daniel's fault for looking so handsome as they drifted beneath the trees, moving in and out of the sunlight. He wore no jacket and his sleeves were short, leaving no doubt of the spare, hard lines of his body, the broad chest and narrow hips. He controlled his horse easily, with slight movements of his muscular thighs that held her attention even while she knew that a wise woman would blank him out, for her own sake.

It was a shame, she thought. So much masculine power and beauty was destined for an athlete, a dancer, or a trapeze artist. One thing was for sure. It was wasted on a king.

CHAPTER FOUR

THAT night Lizzie was about to go to bed when there was a knock on the door to the secret passage.

'It's Daniel,' came a quiet voice from behind.

She slid back the bolts and he stepped into the room, still in white tie and tails from a reception at a foreign embassy. He looked pale and drawn, as though his mind was troubled.

'I've brought you something,' he said, giving her a large brown envelope.

'The letters,' she breathed, exploring.

'Four of them, to start with. You might tell me if you recognise Dame Elizabeth's writing.'

She settled down on the sofa and began to go through them like a treasure hunter who'd just struck gold.

'I don't really know her writing,' she said regretfully. 'In her last years she had arthritis in her hands and never wrote anything down if she could help it. This could be hers. I'm not sure.'

The letters were touching. A gentle, eager soul breathed through the words. This was a woman with a great, tender heart, full of love for one man.

'My goodness,' she breathed. 'I'd really love to—' She checked herself on the verge of saying she'd love to see the other side of the correspondence. It would be silly to throw away her ace while she was winning.

'Love to—?' Daniel asked.

'Love to see the rest of the letters.'

'This is all you get for the moment.'

She began to read the four letters slowly. They were not

only loving but also frankly sensual in a way that made her revise her opinion of Alphonse.

'I wish I'd known your grandfather,' she murmured. 'He can't have been the stick-in-the-mud everyone thought, or no woman would have written to him like this.'

'I beg your pardon!' Daniel said frostily. 'I resent the term "stick-in-the-mud".'

'Sorry,' Lizzie said quickly. 'But you know what I mean.'

'I don't think I do. He was a man I greatly admired—'

'But don't you realise that now you've got another reason to admire him? If he could inspire this kind of love he must have been quite a man. Listen...'

'"*You have given me a reason to live. We are so far apart and see each other so little, and yet you are with me every moment because you're never absent from my heart.*"'

From another letter Lizzie read, '"*I can feel you with me now, your body against mine, your loving still part of me, and I wonder how I lived before we met. To me the world is a beautiful place because you are in it. Whatever happens from now on, I shall say my life was worthwhile, because I was loved by you.*"'

She stopped. After a moment some quality in the silence made her look up to find him staring into space. He looked stunned.

'Daniel,' she said, laying her hand over his.

He didn't look at her. His eyes were fixed on something she couldn't see. Perhaps his grandfather. Perhaps himself.

'I read that letter earlier,' he murmured. 'But I barely noticed those words. When you read them—it's different— I hear them for the first time—almost as though you—'

He stopped, suddenly self-conscious.

'You're right,' he went on after a moment. 'How little I really knew him! I admired him, but I was in awe of him, just as my own children are of me. He seemed so stiff and remote. But he couldn't have been if a woman could write such words to him.'

He gave a wry laugh. 'What do we ever know of another person? I wanted to be like him, and now I discover that I never can be. He was a man who could inspire a woman to say that the world was beautiful because of him. And I know, if I'm honest, that no woman has ever said or even thought that about me.'

'What about your wife?' Lizzie asked.

'I married when I was nineteen. She was twenty-four. We weren't in love. It was a state marriage, and we were raised to the idea of duty.'

'But didn't you ever fall in love?'

'She was in love with someone else. We didn't talk about it. Now I look back, we didn't talk about anything, which may be why we managed to remain on cordial terms until she died. If people don't talk to each other, there's nothing to quarrel about.'

'You poor soul,' Lizzie said, meaning it.

'She's the one you should feel sorry for. She was forced to separate from the man she loved and marry a silly boy. She suffered an arid marriage with only her children to console her, and died before her life could get any better.'

'How did she die?'

'A fall from her horse. She was a reckless rider. Maybe she was trying to ease the frustrations of her life.' He gave a bitter laugh, directed at himself. 'You should have heard my romantic notions as a bridegroom. Despite the odds, I'd convinced myself that we might fall in love. I'd have gladly loved her. She was beautiful. But the other man was always there in her heart, and I never had a chance.'

'Did you know who he was?'

'Oh, yes, he was a splendid fellow, just right for her. A nervous teenager had no chance of winning her heart. I honour her for her fidelity to me. I know she never wavered. But, poor woman, it was a bleak business for her!'

'And for you,' Lizzie said sympathetically.

The picture he'd painted for her was vivid: the lonely boy, longing for some love in a world that had given him none and finding only a wife as deprived as himself. The handsome, apparently confident man before her was a shell. Inside him the 'nervous teenager' still lived, and probably always would, unless another woman's touch could heal his wounds.

Thinking of nothing but to comfort him, she laid her hand on his cheek, searching his face. He raised his eyes to hers and she was shocked at their defencelessness. They were on his ground. By all the rules he should be in control. But something in that letter had broken his control by revealing his own loneliness to him in cruel colours. No woman found the world beautiful because he was in it, and the knowledge broke his heart. Now he was reaching out blindly to her in his need, and she responded with her own need.

For she was as vulnerable as he. Bess had said she was too armoured, implying that if she didn't soon give a man her heart—all of it, with nothing held back—Lizzie was in danger of becoming hard. Her head told her that Daniel could never be the right man. She'd meant only to entice him into letting her win their duel of wits, but suddenly everything was different. She ached for him. She longed to ease his sadness, and everything went down before that. All self forgotten, caring only for him, she put her arms about him.

His own arms went about her at once, and they stood together in a long, close embrace. At first he didn't try to kiss her, but buried his face against her as though finding there some long sought refuge.

'Lizzie,' he whispered, then again, 'Lizzie, Lizzie…' Just

her name repeated over and over, as though the very sound was a spell to ward off evil.

It was sweet to hold him, feeling the warmth of his body mingle with her own, and for the moment that was all she asked. Then she felt the change that came over him as his lips found her neck and began to bestow soft kisses. She sighed with pleasure and began to wreathe her fingers in his hair, turning her neck this way and that to tempt his mouth.

Lower the trail went, down her neck to her almost exposed breasts in the low-cut nightdress, lower still, lower, and every fibre of her being was crying *yes*. She would be cautious another time. This was the man she wanted.

He raised his head. She could feel him trembling. 'You make it very hard to remember that I'm a man of honour,' he growled.

'Perhaps you remember that too often. Is being a man of honour so important?'

'It has to be—it must be—' he said, as if trying to convince himself. He took her face between his hands, speaking softly and with sincerity. 'Lizzie, will you believe me? I didn't come here tonight meaning this to happen.'

'Yes, I believe you.' It was true. Beneath the regimented exterior was a man who could be impulsive. 'It doesn't matter. Don't plan everything. Let things happen to you. It'll be all right. Trust me—trust me—'

And then she felt him freeze suddenly.

'What did you say?' he asked in a strange voice.

'Trust me.' She kissed him playfully. 'Don't you think you could trust me now?'

Bewildered, she knew that a change had come over him. He almost snatched his hand out of hers.

'It isn't that,' he said, sounding as though he spoke with difficulty. 'But I—I really shouldn't be here. This isn't right.'

'I see.' Her eyes flashed. 'Then you don't trust me. How stupid of me to forget.'

'Lizzie, please, it isn't that. It's just that I—I can't explain.'

'Or you don't need to. You lured me here as an enemy, and I'm still an enemy, aren't I? What a pity you confided so much to me tonight. And me a historian! Who knows who I'll tell? Or what indiscreet notes I might make.'

He was pale. 'Will you?'

'Of course not. *You shouldn't have asked me that!*'

'I didn't mean to. I don't know what came over me—at least, I can't explain—'

'I think you already have.'

His tone became more distant. 'There's still a lot we don't know about each other, and perhaps we should both be careful.'

She matched his distant tone with one of her own. 'I think Your Majesty had better leave.'

'Yes, perhaps I should.'

He gave her a small, correct little bow, and went out through the secret door.

She hurried after him and slammed the bolts shut. Then she leaned against the door, resisting the impulse to call him back.

The next morning Frederick brought her a large bag containing the rest of Liz's letters, explaining that he was acting on the King's instructions. His Majesty had left the palace unexpectedly to visit Helmand, his private estate a hundred miles away, and would be gone for some time.

After that she lived in limbo. She didn't know how long Daniel would be away, or whether he meant her to leave before he returned. She only knew that she was furious with him, insulted by him, and yearned for him.

The letters were a goldmine, but a frustrating one. Liz

must surely be Dame Elizabeth, since the pattern of her life seemed to follow the Dame's so exactly. But although there were a thousand hints, there was still no certainty.

The more she read the more she longed for Daniel to be there. There was such love in these pages, and with every passing day she felt an affinity with the writer. 'Liz' had seen an aching need beneath Alphonse's forbidding exterior that had called forth her love and protectiveness. That was their secret. In the world's eyes he was a man of power, but it was she who had protected him.

Daniel was Daniel and not Alphonse, and history never actually repeated itself. But he'd been moulded by the same conditions as his grandfather and left emotionally adrift in the same way. And she knew now that something in him had called to her from the first moment.

Several times she rode with the children. They seemed to like her, and she found them increasingly easy to talk to. Even Sandor's quicksilver temper was controlled in her presence, Elsa was showing signs of a pretty wit, and Felix was beginning to come out of his shell.

They were walking through the woods one afternoon, with Sandor telling them all a funny story, when a sound made them all look up. Daniel was walking through the trees. He wore an informal opennecked shirt, and had something in his arms that squealed and squirmed. Closer inspection revealed it to be three puppies, each about eight weeks.

'A bitch whelped in the Helmand stables a while back,' he said. 'Here you are. One each. Now, be off with you.'

Shouting joyfully, the children took charge of the wriggling bundles, and scampered away.

Daniel stood looking at Lizzie. She hadn't taken her eyes from him since the first moment. Nor had she been able to move. But suddenly movement returned to her. He opened his arms and she threw herself into them.

'I've missed you,' he said between kisses. 'I went away from you, but it did no good. You came with me. You've been with me all the while. You won't go away.'

It was the same with her, and she knew he understood her without words.

'You're in my heart for always,' he said. 'At first I thought you might leave while I was gone, and it would be better for both of us if you did. But this morning I awoke in the early hours and I was so afraid in case you'd left that I had to come home. Kiss me, *kiss me.*'

She responded wholeheartedly, throwing her arms about his neck and giving herself up to the sensation of loving and being loved.

'I've so much to say to you, Lizzie, and you—have you nothing to say to me?'

'Oh, yes, so much.' She took his hand and began to draw him deeper into the wood.

But when he took her in his arms again she discovered that there was nothing to say, or at least nothing that couldn't wait. They clung together like people who'd narrowly avoided falling into an abyss.

A giggle from nearby made them both swing around quickly.

'What are you three—?' Daniel began to yell. Then the urgent pressure of Lizzie's hands checked him. 'I thought you'd gone,' he said, sounding resigned.

'We're sorry, sir,' Felix said quickly. His laugh had faded and he looked anxious.

'You're not annoyed, are you?' Lizzie muttered, so softly that only he could hear.

'No, I'm not annoyed.' Something about their tense faces seemed to get through to him because he added quickly, 'I'm not angry. Really.'

They visibly relaxed and the smiles began to creep back

to their faces, but cautiously, as though ready to vanish again in an instant.

'We came back to say thank you for the puppies,' Sandor said.

'Have fun with them. But you look after them yourselves. You feed them, clean up after them.'

Sandor frowned. 'But there are servants—'

'No servants, *you* do it.' Then Daniel grew still and raised his head, as though listening for silent music in the air. Lizzie held her breath, sure that she knew the thought that had come to him. She was certain of it when he added, 'If you don't feed those dogs, nobody does. So their lives are in your hands.'

The children nodded eagerly and raced off. But when they'd gone Daniel frowned, saying, 'Why did I say that? Of course they haven't got time to—'

'Yes, they have,' Lizzie said, clasping his hand. 'You did the right thing. Perhaps we'd better get back.'

'Yes, we don't want any more little spies,' he said, moving off, still with her hand in his.

That evening she dined with Daniel and the children. It was a happy party, with everyone more relaxed than Lizzie had ever seen them. They kept to safe topics, like dog care, and to Lizzie's surprise Daniel proved an expert.

'I had to care for my own dog when I was a child,' he explained.

'But suppose you had to be away, sir?' Felix asked, frowning.

Daniel winced. 'I'd rather you didn't call me sir.'

'But you've never said anything before,' Sandor pointed out.

He looked surprised. 'I've never noticed before.'

'But what shall we say instead?' Elsa wanted to know.

That confused them, making Lizzie realise that the next step was still a big one.

'Let's sort it out later,' she said quickly. 'Felix wants to know what you did about the puppy when you were away.'

'Then I could delegate someone to do it for me, but it was my job to pick them and explain everything.'

'Father!' Sandor said suddenly. 'Or Poppa. Or Papa.'

'Dad? Daddy?' Lizzie said, then cunningly corrected herself, 'No, I shouldn't have said that. They're *much* too informal. Quite improper.'

'Not at all,' Daniel said at once.

They finally settled on Dad for the boys and Daddy for Elsa. Daniel's eyes met Lizzie's across the table, silently smiling, telling her he understood her little trick.

When the youngsters had gone to bed Daniel said, 'Did you get what I left you?'

'The rest of the letters? Yes, thank you. It was wonderful of you.'

'Did you make anything of them?'

'A good deal, and I think you did too.'

He shrugged. 'I must confess I haven't read them all in detail, just well enough for a general idea of what they were.'

'I think you noticed more than you realise.'

'What do you mean?'

'Come with me and I'll show you.'

In her room she unlocked the drawer where she kept all the letters, and took out one of the first. 'Tell me about the dog you looked after,' she said.

'He was called Tiger. A stupid name because he was just a scruffy mongrel who wandered in one day and attached himself to me. You should have heard the commotion. Only a pedigree animal was suitable for the Crown Prince. But my grandfather let me keep him. He said—'

'Yes?' Lizzie asked.

Speaking as in a dream, Daniel replied, 'He said, "He's your responsibility. If you don't feed him, nobody else will. His life is in your hands." So that's why—today, when I said those words—'

'You were remembering when you last heard them.'

'Yes, I see that, but what does this have to do with a letter?'

'Look at that,' she said, holding one out to him. 'Halfway down the page.'

And there it was, in Liz's words.

> *You talk about teaching Daniel responsibility, but you mean lectures and theory. Give the poor child a dog and let him choose it for himself. He will learn more about responsibility from a creature he loves, and who depends on him entirely, than from all the lessons in books.*

'So that was why he did it,' Daniel said, sitting slowly on the bed, his attention riveted on the paper in his hand. 'It came from her. Then I'm in her debt for years of happiness. And she was right, of course. It was all here, but when I first glanced over this letter I missed it.'

'You weren't ready. Not like now.'

'I really hope Liz is your great-aunt. Not that there's any real doubt of it, but I'm beginning to understand so much— how he depended on her. She must have been the most important person in his life, just as you—' He stopped and looked at her. 'Lizzie, darling, I'm not imagining this, am I?'

'Imagination?' she teased. 'You?'

'No, I haven't much. So I couldn't have imagined that you feel for me as I feel for you. Could I?' He was pleading.

'No,' she said seriously, 'you didn't imagine that.'

He dropped the letter so that it fell, unheeded, to the

floor. He seized her against him like a man just released from prison. His kisses too had the desperation of sudden freedom, shot through with dread lest the precious gift be snatched away. And behind that lay the eagerness of a boy exploring love, almost as a new adventure. She kissed him back in reassurance, but gradually that gave way to the thrills that were coursing through her. He was the man she loved, but he was also the most sexually attractive male animal that it had ever been her privilege to encounter. She'd sensed that at the ball, when she'd first felt his arms about her, and everything since then had been a matter of waiting to tie up the loose ends.

Suddenly he stopped, holding her face between his two hands, whispering, 'Are you sure? Are you quite sure, Lizzie? Don't feel you have to just because I—because of this place and all the trappings.'

She loved him for his doubts. In the past he'd shown her the arrogance of power. Now he trusted her with the humility deep inside him.

'Are you sure?' he repeated again. 'It has to be *me*, for myself alone. I don't want it any other way.'

'Just you,' she promised. 'There's nobody else in my heart, and there never will be again.'

She slipped out of her robe and nightdress so that he could see all the beauty she brought him. She knew her nakedness was magnificent, but at this moment she only cared for it as a gift for the lonely, doubt-ridden man who'd taken refuge in her heart.

And it would be a true refuge for him, she vowed as he lay down beside her on the bed. Whatever the future held, whatever price she had to pay for loving him—and it might be a great one—she would say it was all worth it if she could give him any happiness.

From the way he made love she could tell that the last of his doubts still lingered. There was about him a serious intentness that was beautiful here and now. But far back in her mind she made a note that in future she must teach him how to be a little light-hearted.

No woman could have asked for a more tender or considerate loving, but beneath it she could sense the vigour, sternly leashed back for her sake. The knowledge was a new excitement, a promise for the future. Next time they made love he wouldn't hold it back; she would see to that. But for now they were getting introduced, delighting in what they found, joyful in each other. Only at the last moment did his passion slip beyond his control, and he claimed her with a fierceness that she willingly matched.

There was a long silence then, broken only by breathing and the soft sound of their heartbeats fading. Daniel kissed her and drew her close.

'Thank you,' he murmured.

She gave a chuckle, full of pleasure and satisfaction. 'I think I should be thanking you. That was the nicest thing that's ever happened to me.'

'I want to toast you in champagne.'

'So let's send for some.'

'You mean I should make the call from your room? That would really give them something to talk about.'

'No, I will.' She lifted the house phone and made the order. 'You stay here while I wait for it in the sitting room.'

The champagne arrived five minutes later. Lizzie dressed soberly and closed the door into her bedroom.

'There's only one glass,' she said, bringing everything in a moment later. 'I could hardly ask for two, but I think there are some in that cupboard.' She eyed him, lying naked on the tumbled bed. 'If you lie like that I shall forget all about champagne.'

'Good,' he said, grinning. 'Why are you wearing so much?'

She laughed and tossed her clothes aside while he poured two glasses.

They toasted each other, then Daniel said, 'There must be something else. Let's drink to a bargain well sealed. Except that you haven't kept your side yet.'

'How do you mean?' she asked, trying to sound casual, although she sensed doom creeping up on her. However she'd pictured the moment of truth, it hadn't been like this.

'"I'll show you mine if you'll show me yours,"' he quoted. 'That was the deal. What have you done with Alphonse's letters? Oh, never mind; I'm feeling too happy to worry about that. I just want to think about you. Tomorrow will do for the letters.'

'Yes,' she said, relieved. 'Tomorrow.'

But something in her voice struck his ears strangely. He frowned and looked curiously at her face.

'You have got them safe, haven't you, darling?'

Oh, heck! she thought. Why now?

'You have, haven't you, Lizzie?'

'I thought you said you didn't want to talk about this now?'

'Yes, but you've got me worried. *Lizzie*—'

'Daniel, I told you right from the start that I don't have those letters.'

He looked at her quizzically. 'But of course you have them. You as good as told me—' He caught her eye and said slowly, 'What have we been talking about all this time?'

She took the precaution of rising and moving away, unaware that her shape was distracting Daniel from what he was pursuing. Almost, but not quite.

'Evidently we haven't been talking about the same thing,' she observed.

'You knew I was offering a bargain.'

'And you knew I didn't have them. I told you that in this very room.'

'Yes, but then you—' He rose from the bed and began to follow her. 'Then you—'

'Eased up on the denials a little,' she told him, bland-faced.

He advanced purposefully on her. 'You scheming, two-faced little—'

She backed away. 'Now Daniel—'

'Your Majesty!'

'Rats! If you want to be called Your Majesty, put something on first.'

'Don't change the subject.'

She chuckled. 'There's only one subject that interests me at the moment. You too, from the look of it.'

One glance down at himself was enough to make him accept the inevitable.

'We'll talk later,' he muttered, lifting her right off her feet and tossing her so that she landed sprawling on the bed.

'All right, my love,' she gasped as he dived and landed on top of her. 'Anything that you—mmm!'

CHAPTER FIVE

SHE began a double life. By day she was the historian
working seriously on the Voltavian archives. If she met
Daniel in the presence of anyone else she would address
him as 'Your Majesty' the first time, and 'sir' after that, as
did his courtiers.

But at night she called him Daniel, and laughed as she
melted in his arms. Their loving was passionate, and full
of joy, and afterwards, as he lay sleeping in her arms—for
he always slept first—she would hold him protectively and
wonder if this was how Liz had felt with Alphonse. And
then she knew that was impossible, because no woman in
the world had felt the special joy that was hers.

After the first explosion he'd accepted the fact that she
couldn't produce Alphonse's letters with wry humour. It
delighted her that he had managed to laugh about it.

'You got the better of me,' he said without rancour. 'But
you wait and see. I'll get even.'

'I'm looking forward to it,' she teased.

When she was there he could enjoy a family evening,
and even displayed a talent for playing the piano that none
of his children had known about before.

They confided this to her when Daniel was out of ear-
shot. They revealed also, without exactly knowing they
were doing so, that their mother had drummed into their
head that he was their king first and their father second.
With herself, she had stressed, it was the other way around.

Daniel might regard his late wife generously but Lizzie's
thoughts were less charitable. Serena had been so posses-
sive about her children that she'd bolstered her own posi-

157

tion at her husband's expense, and everyone was suffering
for it now.

Once, when the palace was quiet, he showed her where
he lived, and she was struck by the contrast between the
magnificent bedroom where the king officially slept and the
little monastic cell where he actually passed his nights—
those that he didn't spend with her.

'Who's this?' she asked, looking at a small painting on
the wall. It showed a man in Voltavian military uniform,
but with a gentle, unmilitary face, on the verge of a smile.

'That's my great-uncle, Carl. Alphonse's younger
brother. He was a dear fellow, everybody loved him.
There's a story that the only reason Alphonse married
Princess Irma was to clear the way for Carl to marry the
woman he loved. She was the daughter of a lawyer, respectable and a lady, but this was seventy years ago, when
it was unthinkable for a prince to make such a marriage.
And Carl was next in line to the throne, after Alphonse.

'So Alphonse married and had a son, and then the way
was clear for Carl. He renounced his rights of succession,
married his lady, and they lived very happily for fifty
years.'

'What a charming story. And Alphonse really made a
dutiful marriage just to help Carl?'

'So they say. My grandfather would never confirm or
deny it. But Carl was very dear to him, and his happiest
times were spent visiting the family. Mine too. They always
seemed so happy. Carl was a wise man to marry where his
heart led him.'

'But he did it at someone else's expense,' Lizzie pointed
out. 'Your grandfather couldn't have done the same. Nor
could you.'

Daniel was studying the picture. 'I think I could—now,'
he said. 'I've made one state marriage, given my country
three children. Next time I shall please myself.'

He wasn't looking at her as he spoke—almost deliberately, it seemed to her. She drew a sharp breath at what he might be implying, but before she could reply a buzzer went to summon him to deal with an unexpected crisis. Lizzie had to leave and it was the following evening before she saw him.

He didn't raise the matter again, and she wondered if she'd misunderstood him. Or perhaps he really had meant what she hoped, and then caution had checked him. The thought that they might actually be able to marry was too wonderful to be believed. She wouldn't let herself dwell on it.

Their secret life was charmingly domestic, although Daniel observed that it sometimes made him feel like a character in a French farce. In the morning she was always the first up, slipping out to the sitting room where the newspapers had been quietly laid out by Frederick. Breakfast of rolls and orange juice was served in the same fashion, with Daniel discreetly out of sight behind the bedroom door. And if anyone noticed that Lizzie's food consumption had recently doubled, nobody mentioned it.

They would enjoy breakfast together, lingering until the last moment, until he had to present himself to his court and she must go to the library, and they would look forward to their meeting in the afternoon when they rode with his children.

The morning papers came in three languages, and while with Lizzie Daniel would particularly enjoy reading the English ones, giving some trenchant opinions on what he read there.

'You should see what they say here,' he said one morning. 'I know there isn't a word of truth in it, but what can I—? Lizzie? My darling? What is it?'

She forced herself out of a sad dream and gave him a forced smile. 'Nothing,' she said.

'Don't say "nothing" when it makes you look like that.'

'All right.' She showed him what she'd been reading. The picture of a handsome young man, with a daredevil face, stared out from the paper. The caption read, *Toby Wrenworth killed in motorcycle race.*

Daniel felt as though something had struck him in the chest. He could barely force himself to ask, 'He means something to you, this man?'

'He did once. We were married for a couple of years.'

'Married?'

'I was eighteen and he was handsome and dashing. Auntie warned me against it, but I wouldn't listen. I was so sure I could make him settle down. Of course he didn't. He got bored and took off, and we were divorced. He was only happy taking insane risks. It was only a matter of time before this happened.'

'Did you stay in touch?'

'No. I haven't spoken to him for years. It was all over long ago.'

'But he's remained in your heart?' He was watching her face intently.

'Not him so much as the memories of the happiness we shared. But it was a very short happiness. I was a stupid, ignorant girl or I'd have known I couldn't change him.'

He wished he'd known that stupid, ignorant girl who'd given her whole heart to a man who hadn't valued it. What had she been like in the flush of her first love? His longing to know that, to have been the man who inspired her first young passion, was so intense that for a moment he couldn't speak.

'Don't,' he said, tossing the paper aside and taking her face between his hands. 'Forget him. Look at me.'

She did so, and tried to smile. But it was an unconvincing smile and she saw the shadow of fear cross his face.

'It's all right,' she tried to reassure him. 'I just need to be alone for a while.'

'I have to go, but I'll see you this afternoon—hell, no, I've got meetings all day, and tonight I have to attend the opera.'

'Late tonight, then,' she said.

She spent the day wandering alone in the woods, thinking about Toby. The boy she'd known had been gone even before his death; she could see that from the face in the paper. It was a hard-bitten man who looked out from the front page, and the text made it clear that he'd cared for nothing and nobody except riding his powerful machine in races. Somewhere in the background was a discarded girlfriend and two illegitimate children. The Dame had been right all along. All teeth and trousers. And selfish with it.

Toby had changed her, teaching her the value of keeping her heart to herself, and so, in his way, he'd helped to bring her to this point. She had a heart to give to the one man who mattered, because after that first fling she'd never wasted it again. Her sadness was all for Toby, who'd loved life and lost it while she was preparing to move on to a new life.

It was nearly two in the morning before Daniel came to her, and she could see in his face that his day had been wretched. Years had left him skilled in concealing his feelings, but now they burst out in the first moment.

'Tell me the worst,' he said harshly. 'You still love him, don't you? You've been trying to put him behind you, but you can't.'

'Darling, that's not true.'

'I think it is. That's why you play with men so easily—because you couldn't have the one who mattered. But who do you make love with? When you lie in my arms whose face do you see?'

Suddenly she understood. 'No, you've got it all wrong,' she said, giving him a little shake. 'It isn't happening again, I promise. I'm not Serena, pining for another man.'

He gave a shaky laugh. 'Am I that transparent?'

'Just a little.'

'I thought you were all mine. If I discovered that you weren't, my life would be dark again. And that would be hard to bear when you've shown me the light.'

'I *am* all yours,' she promised. 'I've been over Toby for years. It was just a shock to read about his death like that. I don't dream of him. I dream of you.'

He relaxed in her arms and allowed himself to be reassured. Instead of taking him straight to bed Lizzie ordered a light meal and they sat and talked about nothing very much. It was being together that mattered, and when she could feel that he was calmer and happier, then she took him to bed and loved him tenderly.

As they lay together afterwards he said, 'If I'd known I was going to fall in love with you, I'd have run for my life.'

'Love?' she asked in a soft murmur. 'Is this love?'

'Don't you feel that it is?'

'Yes, I do.' She buried her face against him, whispering, 'And I'm so happy now.'

Next morning he had to leave her earlier than usual for a meeting with his Prime Minister. Before going he said, 'Tonight will be special. I have a surprise for you.'

'A surprise? Oh, tell me now,' she begged eagerly.

'Then it wouldn't be a surprise. I don't want to spoil it, but it's something that will mean a lot to you.' He sighed, kissed her tenderly, and then again. 'If I don't leave you now I won't be able to. Goodbye, my darling, until tonight.'

When he'd gone she had a bracing shower. As she was drying herself her phone rang. She answered eagerly, expecting to hear Daniel's voice. But it was a stranger, and as she listened her smile faded.

She dressed quickly and called Daniel. 'I have to leave, right now,' she said.

'You can't leave me,' he said, becoming imperious in a moment. 'I won't let you go, ever. Wait there.' He hung up before she could reply.

He was with her in a moment. 'What is this nonsense about leaving?'

'I'll come back when I can, but I have a sick friend who needs me. It's Bess. I told you about her. She's had a heart attack and the hospital sent for me. I'm all she has.'

'Forgive me,' he said at once. 'I was being selfish. It's so hard to part with you when I've only just discovered you. But you must go at once. My own plane will take you—'

'No need, darling. There's a flight in an hour, and if I go now I might just catch it.'

'Don't worry. I'll call the airport. It won't leave without you.'

She gave a shaky smile. 'What it is to be a king.'

'It's only valuable to me if I can use it to make your life a little easier. But before you go there's something I want to say—you must understand—'

She waited, but after hesitating for a long moment he sighed and said, 'Never mind. This isn't the moment. But remember that I love you whatever—whatever happens.'

'Darling, whatever's the matter?'

He put his arms about her. 'Promise me that you'll return. You won't just abandon me.'

'How could I do that when I love you so much? I'll be thinking about you.'

'And I,' he said, 'will start to think about you the moment we say goodbye. Wherever you are, whatever you do,

my thoughts will be with you every moment until you return.'

Felix, Sandor and Elsa came down with her to the palace
car that Daniel had commanded to take her to the airport.
As it drove away she looked back to see them waving, their
faces anxious. Raising her eyes a little, she could see Daniel
motionless at an upstairs window.

Lizzie's return to Voltavia was in stark contrast to her departure. Three days later she arrived without warning,
stormed into her apartment and snatched up the telephone
to call Daniel. The phone was answered by Frederick.

'Kindly tell His Majesty that I want to see him.'

Frederick's gasp was audible down the line. He knew,
as everyone did, that Lizzie was privileged, but even she
couldn't command the King with the snap of her fingers.
He tried to explain this diplomatically, but she steamroll-
ered over him.

'Tell him I've got what he wants,' she said sulphurously.
'That'll bring him.'

She hung up. At the other end of the line Frederick
mopped his brow.

For the next few minutes Lizzie prowled her apartment
like an angry lioness, wondering how her happiness could
have turned to dust so quickly. Her visit to England had
been marked by two discoveries, one of which had filled
her with joy and wonder. The other had filled her with such
profound bitterness that she wondered how she could bear
to see Daniel again, ever.

But she would see him, one last time. She would give
him the thing for which he had schemed and betrayed. Perhaps she would even manage to tell him what she thought
of him, although it would be hard to put the depth of her
misery into words. Then she would leave Voltavia and try
to forget that Daniel existed.

She looked up sharply as the door opened. There he was, smiling as though nothing pleased him so much as the sight of her, although she had rudely summoned him in a way that would once have earned his displeasure. He came towards her, hands outstretched, eyes warm. Lizzie clenched her own hands, forcing herself to remember that this man had deceived her cruelly. Otherwise she might have thought he was regarding her with love.

'You came back quickly,' he said, 'just as you promised. But whatever did you say to poor Frederick to put him in such a fret?' She stared at him, bleak-eyed, and his smile died. 'What is it, my darling?'

'Don't call me that,' she said harshly. 'You can stop the pretence. I know the truth now.'

'Whatever do you mean?'

'Did you think I wouldn't find out that you had my house burgled?'

If she'd had any doubts his sharp intake of breath dispelled them. He was pale and startled, but he knew what she was taking about.

'It's true, then,' she said bitterly. 'You did it. You ordered it. And all the time you— Dear God!' The last words were a cry of anguish.

'Lizzie, please listen to me. It's not as you think.'

She rounded on him. 'Of course it is. It's exactly as I think. I was a fool, but I'm not a fool any more, so don't insult my intelligence.'

The sudden silence was harsh and ugly, unlike the sweet, companionable silences that had fallen between them so often.

'How did you know?' he asked at last, in a voice that seemed to come from a great distance.

'Your operatives were very good, but not quite good enough. A few things were out of place. I noticed because I tend to keep things as my great-aunt left them. I didn't believe it at first, but when I questioned my neighbours I learned a lot. Like that they entered by the front door. That's why nobody was alarmed. They looked so respectable.'

Her eyes were very cold as she said, 'I wondered how they got a key to my house. And then I remembered the ball, and how you danced me along the terrace, taking both my hands so that I had to leave my purse behind. You did the "heady passion" bit very well, I'll give you that. And you judged the time so well. Just long enough for someone to open my purse and take a wax impression of the key.'

She waited to see if he would answer, but he stood silent, looking at her with eyes full of pain.

'But why?' she said at last. 'You could have asked me for those letters when we first met in London. You thought I was negotiating. So why not come right out with it there and then? Why invite me here at all?

'That was the question I should have asked myself a long time ago, but I wasn't thinking straight. And why? Because of all that romantic claptrap you showered on me. There wasn't a word of truth in it. You just wanted me in a daze so that I didn't know whether I was coming or going, because that way you could keep me here as long as it suited you. And I fell for it. Me, who prides herself on her cool, logical mind. I could laugh when I remember how I actually lectured you about the lessons of history, but I forgot the most important one, didn't I? *Put not your trust in princes!*

'And all the time I was here your people were going through my house. You didn't want to buy, you wanted to steal.'

'That's not true,' he said harshly. 'I always meant to pay you for those letters, but I was afraid you might have copies, or keep some back.'

'Oh, boy, you were really thorough, weren't you? You even tried my bank. But I don't have a safety deposit box, as I gather the manager told you. Of course, there are a lot more banks to try. Who knows what I might be hiding in some little out-of-the-way branch—?'

'Stop!' he said harshly. 'I deserve all you say of me, but let me tell you the truth—'

'You don't deal in truth. You're a king; you have other priorities. You as good as warned me about that, and I ignored it because—' She choked suddenly. He reached for her but she turned away quickly, throwing up her hands. 'Because I'm a fool.'

'No, because you love me, as I love you.'

'Oh, please!' she cried. Then her manner changed, became formal. 'Your Majesty can abandon those tactics now. They've served their purpose very nicely.'

'That's enough,' he shouted, seizing her shoulders and giving her a little shake. She tried to pull away but he tightened his hands. 'No, you're going to listen to me. I may not deserve it, but you're going to.'

She stood still in his hands, her eyes burning. 'Get it over with, then. It'll be a relief to us both to be done with this.'

'Everything you say was true about me in the beginning. I didn't treat you well. I mistrusted you, I deceived you, I lured you here and I had you burgled. I thought you were an adventuress and that was the only safe way to deal with you. I'm not proud of it, but I thought it was necessary.

'I was wrong. I came to realise that you weren't as I'd thought. I called my people in London and pulled them off the job.'

'Except that they'd already been through my house by then.'

'Unfortunately, yes. I did what I could. I was in love with you by that time. I tried to tell you about this the day you left, to prepare you. But I lost my nerve. I prayed that you'd never find out how I'd behaved, and that you and I could make a new and honest beginning.'

'But you planned to hide the truth about what you'd done. How honest is that?'

'Not very,' he admitted. 'But I was afraid. I couldn't face the thought of losing you.'

She didn't relent. 'The King is never afraid,' she said. 'You should remember that.'

'I'm afraid now,' he said quietly. 'More afraid than I've ever been in my life. At one time I couldn't have admitted to fear, but now I can. You did that for me. Now I see us drawing further apart and I don't know how to stop it.'

'There *is* no way to stop it,' she said wretchedly. 'And I don't want to.'

'Don't say that.' In an instant his fingers were over her lips, trying to silence the terrible words. But she shook herself free.

'It's too late,' she said fiercely. 'And you don't have to bother any more because I've got what you wanted. Here!' Near her on the floor stood a large canvas bag with two leather handles. She dumped it on the table between them and pulled it open to reveal the contents. Daniel stared at the mountain of papers within. 'There they are,' Lizzie said. 'Take them, and then we need never see each other again.'

'What—are these?'

'Alphonse's letters.'

'You had them all the time?'

'No. Only since yesterday. ''Liz'' gave them to me.'

'But she's been dead for years.'

'No. Dame Elizabeth has been dead for years, but she wasn't ''Liz''. We've all been barking up the wrong tree. It was Bess all the time.

'Her name is Elizabeth too, and people used to call her Liz for short. But Auntie ordered her to change it, because it was confusing to have a Liz and a Lizzie. So she became

Bess, and of course I never knew her as anything else. But your grandfather did. She was always ''Liz'' to him. Look.'

She opened her purse and took out a picture. It was about ten years old, an amateurish family shot, showing the teenage Lizzie with the actress, standing haughtily, every inch the *grande dame*. Standing just behind them was a thin little woman with slightly untidy hair. Her dress was nondescript, her face was bare, its only adornment a cheerful smile. Daniel stared at her in disbelief.

'But she's—'

'Exactly,' Lizzie said. 'She's nothing to look at. Not beautiful or glamorous, not a titled lady or a star, not at all the sort of woman you'd expect to be a king's mistress. And she *was* his mistress. His letters leave no doubt of it.

'She was a servant, illegitimate, and in his world she'd have been called a nobody. But she has a great, generous spirit, and she was the love of his life.

'She's kept her secret all these years. But now she's dying, and when she had that attack she called me home so that she could give me these. She said I could do whatever I liked with them. So here they are. Take them, and forget I exist. You've got all you ever really wanted from me.'

In a daze Daniel began to draw the letters out, recognising his grandfather's handwriting even though there was something subtly different about it. It was larger, freer, and Alphonse, a man of few words, had covered endless sheets of paper, as though pouring out a soul.

Daniel went through one letter after another, glancing at each briefly, just long enough to still the last of his doubts.

'What did she say when she gave them to you?' he asked.

When there was no reply he looked up and found himself alone. Lizzie had gone.

Hurriedly he went out into the corridor, but it too was empty. A dreadful suspicion sent him to the window. She must have had a cab waiting all the time, he realised. All that could be seen of it now was the rear vanishing down the long avenue, until it reached the huge wrought-iron gates.

There was still time to stop her. All he had to do was call the gatekeeper. He reached for the telephone, but then checked himself. The habit of command was strong, but right now a command would lose him everything. Whatever he might say, she did not want to hear.

He stayed motionless, undecided, and as he watched the iron gates opened, the car went through, turned and vanished from sight.

CHAPTER SIX

IT WAS very quiet in the King's private rooms. The great clock in the corner silently proclaimed midnight, and the only sound was the rustling of paper on the big table that had been cleared of everything else. Outside the door Frederick sat with orders to permit nobody to disturb Daniel.

Nothing in his life had ever been so important as what he was doing now, fitting together the letters that had passed between two people for thirty years, until one of them had been cruelly struck down so that he could not even utter his beloved's name. It was more than a correspondence. It was a testimony of powerful, enduring love that awed him as he read.

Lizzie had said there was no doubt that they had been lovers in every sense of the word, and Daniel had already discerned as much from the 'Liz' letters. Yet they were relatively restrained. Alphonse's were totally frank. He had loved this woman with his heart, his soul and his great, vigorous body. He had loved her fiercely, sexually, without false modesty or pride, and she had stimulated him to ignore his advancing years and love her with the urgent desire of a much younger man. Daniel, no prude, found himself blushing at some passages.

Yet this in itself was not the greatest surprise. That had come with the discovery that his grandfather, a strictly traditional man where 'a woman's place' was concerned, had turned to Liz for advice. As time passed she had become more than his lover. She had been his counsellor.

Suddenly Daniel grew still. His own name had leapt out at him from the paper.

I try to do my best by the boy, but what am I to do when he takes such wild ideas into his head? Why piano lessons? He's going to be a king, not join an orchestra.

Daniel read the phrase again and again, and suddenly time turned back and he was a boy of ten, wanting to learn the piano because it was only in making music that he could find the strength to cope with the pressures that were already threatening to crush him. But all authority had lain with his grandfather, who didn't understand, and who was impatient of explanation.

And then, out of the blue, Alphonse had yielded. A fine music master had been engaged and a new joy had entered Daniel's life. Yet even while he'd rejoiced he'd puzzled over his grandfather's *volte face*.

He went to the secret drawer where he'd kept the other side of the correspondence since Lizzie's first departure, yanking it out in a violent movement quite different from his usual restraint. The letters spilled all over the floor and he dropped to his knees, searching as though his life depended on it.

At last he found what he wanted: a letter from Liz in response.

Say yes to what he asks, my dearest. His life will be so hard. Indulge him and make his coming burden a little easier. Let the poor child have some pleasure. However much it is, it still won't be enough.

There was more. For years Alphonse had laid his personal problems in his darling's hands and trusted her answers. Daniel found the story of his childhood and teenage years relived in these letters.

He remembered his father's death. How stiff and distant Alphonse had seemed over the loss of his only son. It was only to Liz that he had released the rage and pain that consumed him. In letter after letter he'd let out a howl of fatherly anguish.

Now he realised how much he'd overlooked when he'd first glanced through these pages. The sight of his own name in Liz's letters gave him a sensation that he'd never known before, and which at first he couldn't identify. But it was a good feeling—of being able to let down his guard in a trusted presence. Where Alphonse had worried how he should rear the future king, Liz had seen only the bereaved child.

He's just a little boy...let him be happy while he can...make him safe...tell him you love him...don't let him be ashamed to cry...be kind to him...be kind to him...

Over weeks, months and years she had counselled love and gentleness to the child.

In Daniel's mind those years were a blur. But now scenes began to come back to him: himself at nine years old, fighting back the tears even in the privacy of his own room, because now he was heir to the throne, and a man, and men didn't cry. Then his grandfather coming in, seeing the tears he was too late to hide. He'd waited to be blamed, but instead the stern face had softened, a kindly hand had rested on his shoulder, and a gruff voice had whispered, 'I know, my boy. I know.'

Other things. The music lessons—understood now for the first time. And Tiger, the mongrel, his own special care and his dearest friend. So much owed to this woman he'd never known.

Daniel took out the picture that Lizzie had left behind. It was hard to see much of Liz, standing in the shadows behind the other two. But he could make out the gentle glow of her face. And suddenly he could identify the unknown feeling that had eased his heart. His mother had died when he was a baby, and he'd never known a mother's love, but over the years and the miles Liz had tried to make up for that lack. And she'd succeeded more than any other woman could have done. Looking at her now, Daniel thought he could understand why.

He hadn't noticed the hours pass until Frederick knocked on the door. He answered it, but didn't allow him in. Frederick was startled at his pallor.

'Speak to my secretary,' Daniel commanded. 'Cancel any appointments I have for tomorrow. Say I'm detained on urgent business. And send me in some food.'

Through the night he worked, and then through the following day. When he came to an end he was unshaven and exhausted. But now he knew what he had to do.

She would sell the house, Lizzie decided as the plane headed back across the English channel. She had kept it almost as the Dame had left it, but now everything would remind her of the man who'd won her love with a lie. Just because she was a historian that didn't mean she must live in the past. With the house gone she would put everything behind her, abandon her book on Alphonse, and find a new life for herself.

Her anger lasted until she was indoors and under the shower. But the hot water couldn't lave her grief away and she let the tears come freely. She was a woman who never cried, but she cried now for the magic that had been a delusion, and for a feeling that she knew would never come again as long as she lived. Tonight she would let herself mourn what might have been. Tomorrow she would put it behind her and become a different woman, a more resolute and, if necessary, a harder one. Her mourning was for that too.

She spent the next day making plans. By evening the house bore a 'For Sale' notice and she told herself that things were proceeding wonderfully. Now all she wanted was to get out of here fast. She obtained some tea chests and began packing things away. With luck she could be out in a few days, leaving an agent to sell the house.

She worked blindly while the thoughts thrummed through her head. Everything that had happened in Voltavia had been an illusion, including Daniel's feelings. She'd been useful to him. Now he had what he wanted, and she was disposable. That was all there was to it. At least she had the advantage of knowing exactly where she stood. As she threw things into tea chests her anger mounted.

Midnight passed, then one, then two in the morning. With her mind in turmoil there was no point in going to bed. She was still working frantically when the front bell rang. She opened the door and at once a hand came through the gap, preventing her slamming it closed.

'Don't shut me out,' Daniel begged. 'Not until you've heard what I have to say.'

'We've said everything. Please go away Daniel. Nothing can make it right, and why bother?'

'Listen to me!' As she turned away he seized her shoulders fiercely. 'You have to.'

'Don't tell me what I have to do. I'm not one of your subjects.' She wrenched free and went into the kitchen to put on the kettle. It was a way of not looking at him. If he saw her face he might also see the leap of joy she hadn't been able to suppress at the sight of him. She thought she'd controlled it now, but she couldn't be sure, and it was wisest not to trust him.

He followed her and stood watching as she moved about. 'Not a word?' he asked at last. 'I turn up at this hour and you're not even curious?'

'What is there to be curious about? I'm sure you snapped your fingers and everybody jumped. Did they hold the plane for you?'

'There wasn't one. I chartered a special plane because all I could think of was getting to you. And I find a "For Sale" sign and you packing to leave.' His voice became tinged with anger. 'You really weren't going to give me a second chance, were you?'

'You don't need a second chance,' she cried. 'You've got everything you wanted. And you were brilliant. I'll give you that. You schemed and manipulated like a pro. But then, of course, you *are* a pro. A king would have to be. Well done, Your Majesty. But don't expect me to applaud and say it's all right.'

'Do you really believe that?' he asked quietly. 'You think there was nothing in my feelings for you but scheming?'

She shrugged. 'Why deny it? It's a perfectly honourable position for a king. Not for a man, of course, but what does that matter? The man can always hide behind the king, and that's what you're good at.'

He was about to hurl an angry reply at her when he caught a look at her face and read in it the misery and exhaustion of the last thirty-six hours.

'I'll never forgive myself for hurting you,' he said. 'It's true I wasn't honest with you at the start, but I swear that was only for a short time. It didn't take me long to see how good and true you are, how much better than my fears. If you'll let me, I'll spend my life making it up to you.'

But his words washed over her. She couldn't answer. She

could only look at him sadly, thinking of the chance that was lost for ever.

'How is Bess?' he asked.

'Holding on, but she's very weak. I'm visiting her today.'

'Good, because it's partly her that I came to see.'

'You can't be serious.'

'I was never more serious in my life. Since you left I've been reading all the letters—both sides of the correspondence, fitted together—and I've seen many things. I've seen that my grandfather wasn't at all the way he seemed, cold and remote. He was a man with a warm heart, which he found hard to show, except to her. But I've seen something else. Lizzie, you must let me meet Bess. I know now that she virtually raised me.'

'Whatever do you mean by that?'

'I mean that she guided my grandfather in his dealings with me. He'd have got everything wrong if she hadn't put him on the right path. I told you about the dog, the music lessons—it was her doing. But for her my life would have been so different, so much harder. She has been almost my mother, and I must thank her while there's still time.'

'She's a very old woman,' Lizzie said slowly. 'She hardly knows what's happening—'

'All the more reason for you to take me to her, today. And there's another reason—something I must tell her before anyone, even before you.'

His voice rang with sincerity but Lizzie was bruised from their last encounter. She searched his face, desperately seeking an answer.

'Lizzie, you must trust me,' he cried passionately. 'I beg you to believe me this one time.'

'Very well,' she said slowly. 'I'll take you to see Bess.'

Bess had come through her heart attack weak but lucid. They found her lying propped up against some pillows. She smiled at the sight of Lizzie, but her smile turned to awe when she saw Daniel. Frail though she was, she instinctively reached out a hand to him, and Daniel took it at once.

'You,' she whispered. 'You—'

Lizzie drew a quick, dismayed breath. 'Bess—it's not—'

'No, my dear, it's all right. I didn't really think—well, perhaps for a moment.'

To Lizzie's pleasure, Daniel sat beside the bed and spoke to Bess quite naturally. 'I believe I look very like my grandfather.'

'A little,' she conceded. Then her eyes twinkled as she added, 'Of course, he was *much* better looking. Just the same, I would have known you anywhere.'

'We have been acquainted for a long time,' Daniel said gently, 'although I've only just found out. It was you who softened his heart—'

'Oh, no,' Bess said quickly. 'He always had a great heart. But it was imprisoned. He used to say that I had set him free.'

'Yes,' Daniel said gravely. 'That's very easy for me to believe—now. Won't you please tell me about him. How did you meet?'

'It was fifty years ago. He came to London for the Queen's coronation, and he went to the theatre one evening. The show was *Dancing Time*, starring Lizzie Boothe. She wasn't Dame Elizabeth in those days, but she was at the height of her fame and beauty. After the performance he came backstage to meet the cast, and I was there too, lurking in the shadows to catch a glimpse of him. He noticed me and made someone bring me forward. My knees were knocking, I was so nervous. But he smiled at me, and suddenly I wasn't afraid any more.'

There was a hint of mischief in Bess's voice as she said, 'After that I was weak at the knees for another reason. He invited himself to lunch next day, and of course he brought an aide, and the aide whispered in my ear that His Majesty would like to speak to me alone. And when I saw him he told me that he loved me. It was as simple as that.'

'But what about the Dame?' Lizzie asked.

'She was our friend,' Bess said at once. 'She let us use her as "cover". It was all right for people to believe he admired her, in a theatrical kind of way. He once said, "I don't mind if people think I'm a glorified stage-door Johnny."'

'My grandfather *said* that?' Daniel asked, startled.

'Oh, yes. He had a very neat line in humour when he was in the mood.'

'I never saw him in that mood,' Daniel said regretfully.

'He kept it for me,' Bess sighed. 'And for the Dame, too, because he was grateful to her for helping us.'

'Didn't she mind?' Lizzie wanted to know.

'Only at first. She had so many conquests, and of course she'd have liked to add his scalp to her belt, for the fun of it. But when she saw how things stood she was very kind. And of course he gave her jewels and flowers, so the world *thought* she had his scalp, and that was really all she asked. She once told me that the situation suited her very well. "All the kudos and none of the inconvenience," was how she put it.'

'What did she mean, "inconvenience"?' Lizzie asked.

Bess paused before saying delicately, 'Well, my dear, contrary to appearances, the Dame wasn't a very *sensual* person. She liked to be admired from a distance. She used to say that frantic passion was all very well in its place, but it made such a mess of the hair. Alphonse was a very *vigorous* man, and I—well, let's just say that I never cared about my hair.'

'You're making me blush,' Daniel murmured.

'Well, it won't do you any harm,' Bess retorted with

spirit. 'I wasn't always a dried-up old stick. And I have a very good memory.' She smiled, but she wasn't looking at them. 'Oh, yes, I remember everything. Everything he ever said to me—everything he did—every kiss—every whisper—'

Lizzie's eyes blurred, for suddenly the years had fallen away from Bess and she was once more the little maid, living in the shadows, in her thirties, thinking she would never know love. But then the most glorious man in the world had come striding into her life, caring nothing for the others but only for her and the special something she had to offer.

'He used to come over here incognito, whenever he could,' she said. 'Once we stole away and went to a fair. Nobody recognised him, and we went around all the stalls. He won this at the coconut shy, and gave it to me.' She pointed to the cheap ring on her finger. 'It was the only jewel I'd let him give me. He wanted to give me some of his family jewels. I couldn't let him, of course—the scandal—so he made a financial settlement on me, so that I should never be in want.'

'So that's how you could afford this place,' Lizzie said.

'That's right. Oh, if you could have seen his face when he told me about the money! He was so afraid that I'd be offended. Money might have meant that I was a certain kind of woman, you see.'

'But a man expects to provide for his wife,' Daniel said. 'And in his heart you were his wife and Queen.'

'That's what he said. We used to talk of the day when I could come to Voltavia and live in a little cottage near him. But it was all a pipe dream. People would have known and looked down on me and, although I wouldn't have minded, he would have minded for me. And besides, I couldn't leave the Dame. She'd been good to me, and she was getting old and blind. He understood that my duty had to come first. He said it made him love me more.

'I used to think that when she no longer needed me I might go out to him at last, and hang what people said. But then he had a stroke. They said it was savage and terrible, cutting him down in a moment, and all communication between us was cut off, so cruelly. He couldn't write to me, and I didn't dare write to him. It was as though he was dead. And yet I knew he was alive, longing for me.'

'He always knew that you loved him,' Daniel said. 'I didn't know anything of this at the time, but I'm certain of this.'

Bess smiled. 'How like him you are. Now I can see it. You have his eyes and his loving heart.' She laid a feeble hand on Lizzie's. 'You're very lucky my dear. When the men of this family love, they really know how to love. It's very exciting.'

Lizzie's eyes met Daniel's. 'Yes, it is,' she murmured.

Daniel took Bess's hands between both his, and spoke very gently. 'I had a special reason for coming to see you. I have a letter—his last letter—one that you never received.'

'I don't understand.'

'He must have been in the middle of writing it and laid it aside because he wasn't feeling well, and the stroke caught him before he could take it up again... At all events, it was found locked away with your letters to him. He never had the chance to finish it, and so you never received it.'

Lizzie stared at him. 'I had no idea...'

'It was the surprise I had for you before you left,' he told her. 'That was how much I'd come to trust you by then, but things went wrong for us.' He took out a sheet of paper and carefully placed it in Bess's hand. 'After all these years, this is his last message to you.'

The old woman's voice was husky. 'I can't see—read it for me, please—'

Daniel moved very close to her and took one of her hands in his.

'"My dearest love,"' he read, '"always dearer to me than anyone else on earth, because you know everything about me, and love me in spite of the worst—my heart is heavy tonight because yesterday we parted. Perhaps it is only for a little while, and we may still hope for the next meeting, in a month, as we discussed. But as I grow older I fear that each parting may be the last, and I may never again have the chance to tell you what you are, and have been to me.

'"And so I set it down, in the hope that when I can no longer say the words it will somehow reach you. Others see you occupying a lowly position, but to me you will always be a great, great lady: the woman who brought my heart to life and showed me what love could be. I lived encased in stone until you broke me free."'

'You sound—just like him,' Bess murmured.

'I was just like him,' Daniel said softly. 'Until my Lizzie came to me. Encased in stone, needing to be set free. But only if she wishes.'

Bess regarded Lizzie with eyes that saw everything. 'Whatever he has done to offend you,' she said shrewdly, 'it is as nothing beside the love that you share. Throw the defences away, my dear. They have no place about your heart.'

'Yes,' Lizzie said with her eyes on Daniel. 'I know that.'

'Finish the letter for me,' Bess pleaded.

'There isn't very much more,' Daniel said, taking up the page again. '"I do not know what the future holds,"' he read, '"But I am certain that it must be a future together. If not in this world, then in another that we cannot even imagine. However long the wait, I shall watch for you with *my arms open and my heart as much yours as on the day—'''* He stopped. 'That's where it finishes.'

'It is enough.' Tears were streaming from Bess's eyes. 'He always promised not to leave me without a last message, and he was a man of his word. Oh, my dears, my dears—if only you could be as happy as I am—'

Two hours later Bess slipped quietly out of life. Daniel and Lizzie were with her as she fell asleep, still holding her beloved's final letter. When they had both kissed her Lizzie took the paper gently from Bess's fingers.

'I'll put it back before the funeral,' she said. 'And it can be buried with her.'

'Would you like to have her taken to Voltavia and placed near him?'

After a moment's hesitation Lizzie shook her head. 'Thank you, but there's no need. I believe that they're together now, and that's what matters.'

'And what becomes of us?'

'What do you want to become of us, my love?'

'Be my wife, and keep me always in your heart, for only there will I be safe.'

Six weeks later King Daniel of Voltavia married Elizabeth Boothe in a small private ceremony, attended only by his children and a few trusted friends. His daughter was a bridesmaid, and his sons, following royal convention, shared the role of groom's supporters.

There was much talk about the King's wedding gift to his bride: a fabulous diamond set, including a tiara, necklace, bracelets and earrings. But nobody knew of his real gift to her: the complete correspondence between King Alphonse and 'Liz', with his permission to publish it as she pleased.

Nor did anybody know that she had thanked him and refused to publish—the first time in Voltavia's history that the King's bride had turned down his wedding gift and made her husband a happy man by doing so.

But Lizzie had one final gift for the man she loved and who loved her beyond anything he could express in words. On their wedding night they stood before the great open fire in his apartment and tossed the letters—every last one—into the flames, watching until there was nothing left.

He took her into his arms. 'No regrets at depriving history?'

'No regrets,' she assured him lovingly. 'We've done them justice. History would never have understood them as we do, and only the future matters now.'

Harlequin Presets°
and
Harlequin Romance°
have come together to celebrate a year of royalty

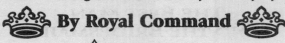 **By Royal Command**

HARLEQUIN°
Romance°

EMOTIONALLY EXHILARATING!

Coming in June 2002
His Majesty's Marriage, #3703
Two original short stories by **Lucy Gordan** and **Rebecca Winters**

On-sale July 2002
The Prince's Proposal, #3709
by **Sophie Weston**

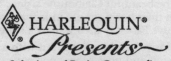
HARLEQUIN°
Presents

Seduction and Passion Guaranteed!

Coming in August 2002
Society Weddings, #2268
Two original short stories by **Sharon Kendrick** and **Kate Walker**

On-sale September 2002
The Prince's Pleasure, #2274
by **Robyn Donald**

**Escape into the exclusive world of royalty with
our royally themed books**

Available wherever Harlequin books are sold.

HARLEQUIN°
Makes any time special °

Liz Fielding

Winner of the 2001 RITA Award for
Best Traditional Romance, awarded for

THE BEST MAN
AND THE BRIDESMAID

Coming soon:
an emotionally thrilling new trilogy from this
award-winning Harlequin Romance® author:

It's a marriage takeover!

Claibourne & Farraday is an exclusive London department
store run by the beautiful Claibourne sisters, Romana, Flora
and India. But their positions are in jeopardy—the seriously
attractive Farraday men want the store back!

It's an explosive combination...but with a little bit of
charm, passion and power these gorgeous men become
BOARDROOM BRIDEGROOMS!

Look out in Harlequin Romance® for:

May 2002
THE CORPORATE BRIDEGROOM (#3700)

June 2002
THE MARRIAGE MERGER (#3704)

July 2002
THE TYCOON'S TAKEOVER (#3708)

Available wherever Harlequin® books are sold.

HARLEQUIN®
Makes any time special ®

Visit us at www.eHarlequin.com

HRBB

Do you like stories that get up close and *personal*?
Do you long to be loved *truly, madly, deeply...*?

If you're looking for emotionally intense, tantalizingly
tender love stories, stop searching and start reading

Harlequin Romance®

You'll find authors who'll leave you breathless, including:

Liz Fielding

Winner of the 2001 RITA Award for
Best Traditional Romance
(The Best Man and the Bridesmaid)

Day Leclaire

USA Today bestselling author

Leigh Michaels

Bestselling author with 30 million
copies of her books sold worldwide

Renee Roszel

USA Today bestselling author

Margaret Way

Australian star with 80 novels to her credit

Sophie Weston

A fresh British voice and a hot talent!

Don't miss their latest novels, coming soon!

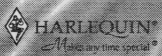

HARLEQUIN®
Makes any time special®